SERIOUSLY SEXY 2

SERIOUSLY SEXY 2

A COLLECTION OF TWENTY EROTIC STORIES

EDITED BY

MIRANDA FORBES

Published by Accent Press Ltd – 2008
ISBN 9781906125868

Reprinted 2011

The stories contained within this book are works of fiction. Names and characters are the product of the authors' imaginations and any resemblance to actual persons, living or dead, is entirely coincidental.

Printed and bound in the UK

Cover Design by
Red Dot Design

Contents

Thanks for the Memory
by Roxanne Sinclair

WEARING NOTHING BUT AN oversized beach towel, Carla grabbed her wash bag and bounced down the two steps of the caravan in France that had been her home for the last week and a half. The sun was already warm even though it was not yet seven o'clock in the morning and she headed to the shower block with the feeling that today was going to be a good day.

She was the only person in the small brick building, probably the first of the day. The smell of disinfectant hung in the air as a reminder of the cleaner who had been there earlier.

She walked into the middle cubicle and allowed the door to close behind her at its own pace. She removed her towel and draped it over the hook on the back of the door, watching the door click shut, she did not lock it.

Walking the three feet from the door to the shower head, she positioned herself under it and twisted the silver knob, bracing herself for what she knew was coming. The first thirty seconds or so was always icy cold but Carla took delight in the way it made her feel.

The initial touch made her catch her breath but she

forced herself to stay under the water. She bounced on her toes without realising it until her body became accustomed to the temperature. Her arms were by her side and her face was turned up to the ceiling. The jet of water landed in the V at the base of her neck and formed tiny rivers that ran down her body on their way to the ground. Her whole body came alive under its icy fingers. Her skin formed goosebumps and tingled. Her nipples were hard and erect.

Carla shook her head. Her auburn hair fanned out like ribbons.

She glanced over her shoulder and grasped the bar of soap from her wash bag by the door. She held the tablet under the water and rotated it between her fingers. A film coated her hands and she rubbed them together to form a thick foamy lather.

She rubbed that foam along the length of her neck. As her hands moved along her upturned throat she could smell a hint of mango from the scented soap She closed her eyes and enjoyed the sensation. She passed one hand briefly over the back of her neck before leaning forward and allowing the water to wash all the foam away.

She worked the soap into another lather and ran one hand over her other arm before repeating the motion with her other hand. With her arms still covered in suds she ran her hands over the wet mounds of her breasts.

Her fingers caressed the underside of each breast before moving over their point and onto the top. Her nipples were still erect and she squeezed them between her fingertips. It was more an act of arousal than hygiene and Carla repeated the whole motion, enjoying the sensation.

Lost in her own world of personal pleasure Carla didn't hear the door open behind her. She sensed someone behind her, but didn't turn around. Instead, she moved her hands over her breasts once more. This time a moan accompanied the action.

Moving very slowly and with her eyes closed, she turned around and realised how disappointed she would be if she found herself face-to-face with the cleaning lady. She kept her eyes closed a second or two longer than she needed to.

When she opened her, eyes a smile formed on her lips. She was not disappointed by what she saw.

'Oh,' she feigned surprise.

He said nothing. His lips were parted in a smile of his own and his eyes rested on her hands which still cradled her breasts. She worked her fingers into the soft flesh and watched him enjoying the show that she was putting on.

Her eyes dropped to the shorts that he was wearing and admired the stalk that had formed. She caught his eyes with hers and indicated that he should lose the shorts. This he did immediately, allowing his cock to bounce free from its prison. It came to rest at an angle about forty-five degrees to his stomach and twitched in anticipation with a life of its own.

Using her head this time, she indicated that he should join her under the spray and he obeyed with a smile. They locked eyes, each defying the other to back away.

Without taking her eyes off his Carla noticed the rise and fall of his Adam's Apple. She felt his breath on her lips. He was breathing harder and faster now.

Carla inched forward until the tips of her nipples touched the soft down that covered his chest. Carla looked into his eyes and knew that he would do whatever she asked him to.

She asked him to wash her by offering him the soap. He understood the silent command and took it from her. He started by rubbing it up and down the right side of her neck in a slow rhythm. He did the same on the other side before resting the soap on the ledge to his right. He then put his hands either side of her neck and made small circular motions with his thumbs before spreading his fingers out wide.

He moved his hands along her shoulders, allowing his fingertips to follow their natural curve. His hands moved down her arms until they reached her elbows, at which point he lifted her arms and moved them above her head. She held them in place and waited for what he would do next.

He copied the motion that she had made a few minutes earlier, rolling the soap between his hands to form a cream. He let the soap slip back onto its ledge and moved the cream from one hand to the other, until he was happy with the amount in each palm.

Smiling widely, he deposited the contents of each hand onto the tip of her breasts, deliberately flicking each nipple as he did so.

He used the ends of his fingers to spread the tiny bubbles over the curve of her breasts. Then, using the heels of his hands, he kneaded the soft orbs. He squeezed them and moulded them; all the time his lips were inches from hers.

She could feel his cock pressing against her and she wanted him badly. The anticipation was almost too much for her. She inched her face closer to his but he backed away, laughing as he did so.

'No.' He spoke for the first time in an accent that Carla couldn't quite place. That single word sent a shudder through her body which exited at that point between her legs. He turned her around so that the water could wash the suds away.

As the water pounded her front, his stiff rod rested in the crack of her arse and she wished he would shove it in her and pound her from the back too. He knew that what she wanted, so he pushed himself closer to her. He ran his hands over her stomach, allowing only the little finger of his right hand to stray anywhere near the line of hair that ran down the crack of her pussy.

Her breath caught in her throat and her head fell backwards onto his shoulder. He pressed his lips to her neck and kissed it, gently at first and then with more ferocity.

She groaned and fell against him as his finger separated her slit and worked its way inside.

'You like?' he asked.

'I like,' she confirmed. So why did he stop? She looked over her shoulder. He turned her around.

'You like this more I think,' he said, and she didn't doubt that she would.

He placed the index finger of his right hand into the V of her throat. Very slowly he moved that finger in a straight line down her body. He didn't deviate from his path as he moved down her breast-bone and over the tiny bulge of her stomach. When he hit her soft mound, he shifted his hand and pushed his middle finger deep inside her.

In-and-out, in-and-out in a slow rhythm, making

sure he caught her clitoris with each movement.

Then the fingers either side of his middle finger also entered her and it wasn't long before she felt the rising of an orgasm, which exploded as a sensation that started between her legs and came out of her mouth as a noise she didn't recognise.

Satisfied with what he had achieved, he stood up straight and slowly put the fingers that had recently been inside her into his mouth, making a noise that said he liked what he tasted.

Now it was Carla's turn to take the lead and she stood aside. She indicated with her head that he should take her position which he did without question. Carla looked down at the penis which was now almost flat against his stomach. She was ready and eager to work.

Her work involved cupping his balls in the palm of her left hand and squeezing gently. Her right hand wrapped itself around his shaft and rubbed. She worked the already exposed tip of his knob between her thumb and forefinger. She could see the state of his arousal in the tiny drop of spunk that escaped onto her fingers.

With a practised move she shifted her hand until he was resting in her palm and she used a pulling rather than rubbing action. All the while his balls were resting in her left hand and she used her painted finger nails to gently scratch them. He enjoyed that part especially.

He let her work him for several minutes, enjoying the rewards of her expert touch before making a noise that sounded something like 'Stop.'

She was surprised by his request but quickly realised that he had something else in mind. He pulled her up and manoeuvred her around the small space until they had changed positions. He indicated with his eyes that she should stand on the tiled ledge that ran either side of the cubicle.

She understood what he wanted and why. She tingled with pleasure at the thought of it. She planted her feet firmly on the ledges and bent her knees slightly so that she would be the right height for him to enter her. He positioned his rod between her legs and let it find its own way to the Promised Land. A couple of small movements later and it was at the rim of her hole.

He punctured her quickly and with a force that pushed her back against the wall. The position of the tap made her arch her back and the water fell between them, splashing onto their bodies as their crotches bounced together.

He grabbed her arse, spreading her cheeks as he pulled her towards him. She raked her fingers through his hair and held onto him.

With each of his moves, up she moved down, increasing the force of each penetration. It wasn't long before she felt the beginnings of another orgasm forming.

When it came, her whole body shuddered and goosebumps formed, causing her to tingle from head to toe. His climax wasn't ready yet and his rhythm never missed a beat. Gradually his pace quickened and his movements intensified. A noise accompanied each thrust now, and Carla noticed that his face had become tight.

Then the tightness was replaced by something else as Carla felt his warm fountain shoot inside her. He entered her a couple more times to make sure that he was empty, before collapsing against her.

Their sated bodies clung together for several minutes under the stream of water. When he fell from her, she felt his juice escape and make its way down her leg. Soon it would be gone the way of the water and the suds that it was mixed with. All that would remain would be the memory.

Phone Jack
by Landon Dixon

MY WIFE AND I recently combined our insatiable desire for oral sex with the titillating world of phone-sex, and we're left to wonder why we hadn't done so a long time ago. To be accurate, when I say phone-sex, I don't mean me phoning up my wife and talking dirty to her, or vice versa, or getting a third party to do it; what I mean is that my wife and I have sex while one of us is on the phone. It's added an exhilarating rush to our already intense oral activities.

It started one day when I was home on vacation. I was waiting for Vicky, my wife, to finish some work so that we could head out to the beach. She was putting in a couple of hours at her home-based public relations firm, following things up with a few of her clients. I was amazingly horny that morning, considering that Vicky and I had already engaged in a wicked sixty-nine just before the crack of dawn, with Vicky swallowing what seemed like half a gallon of my ejaculate while I lapped up an equally copious quantity of her tangy juices. It had been quite the pre-breakfast treat, and had left me hungry for more.

I tip-toed into her basement office while she was

talking on the phone, surprising her by putting my hands on her bare shoulders and then starting to massage her neck and shoulders. She glanced back at me and smiled, then covered the mouthpiece on the phone and said, 'It's Cathcart,' and rolled her eyes.

Lyndon Cathcart owned a furniture store downtown, and Vicky did a fair amount of advertising work for him. He was notoriously long-winded, forever spouting off about some new scheme to sell his merchandise, so I knew that Vicky was going to be tied up for quite some time. But instead of releasing her buff shoulders from my grasp and leaving her to deal with her vocal client, I decided to have some fun. Just touching her warm, smooth skin had aroused my cock yet again, and its need for release overrode her need for privacy.

I continued rubbing her sun-kissed shoulders, gently probing her long, slender neck with my fingers, and then I bent down and nuzzled the side of her neck, kissed and licked her soft, scented skin. She giggled and tried to shrug me off, but I wouldn't be discouraged. I ran my tongue up and down the side of her neck, under her shiny, black curtain of hair and behind her ear.

She moaned softly when my wet tongue licked at the back of her delicately shaped ear. Then she quickly covered the receiver with her hand again. 'What are you doing, Jim?' she asked, her face flushed.

'Helping you deal with your business worries, my dear,' I whispered, before replacing words with action and swirling my tongue around inside her rose petal of an ear.

'Jesus,' she murmured. 'No, no, Mr Cathcart, I

didn't say anything. I was just jotting down some notes on that billboard idea of yours. Please, continue.'

I took that last part as being directed at the both of us, so, as Cathcart droned on, I tongued Vicky's earlobe, then caught it between my lips and tugged on it. I pushed the straps of her tank-top off her shoulders and caressed the golden flesh of her arms and chest. I slid my hands underneath the thin fabric of her top and fondled her naked breasts.

'Yes,' she whimpered; Cathcart thinking, no doubt, that she was agreeing with one of his 'swell' ideas.

I stroked her firm, high breasts; cupped and squeezed them, played with her nipples, her buds rapidly flowering to their full half-inch length as I rolled and lightly pinched them. I kissed her neck more urgently, bit into her delicate flesh as I felt up her boobs.

'Don't stop,' she breathed, her head lolling back on her shoulders, basking in the erotic sensations that my loving hands and lips were eliciting. She pressed the phone hard against her ear, the mouthpiece tilted away from her mouth, her hand shaking, her knuckles white.

I spun the chair around so that she was facing me, and she searched my fiery eyes with her azure eyes, and quickly realised that I meant to have her pussy – meant to eat her out and make her come right then and there, while she talked on the phone. I was burning with desire; I wanted, needed to taste her beautiful pussy, lap up her sticky juices all over again. She nodded her head.

After some awkward twisting of the phone cord, I had her top down around her waist, her chest bare and heaving. She was tanned all over from our endless hours spent at the beach, except for a couple of small white triangles on her breasts where her skimpy bikini normally covered her. Her pink nipples jutted out at me, yearning for my hands and mouth.

She slid further down in the chair and I dropped to my knees in front of her, gripped her breasts and without further ado began teasing her sensitive nipples with my tongue. 'God, yes,' she groaned.

'What!? Are you all right, Ms Forzani?' I heard Cathcart ask in his high-pitched voice. 'Are you listening to what I'm saying!?'

Vicky took a deep breath and ran her trembling fingers through her hair as I flicked my tongue against first one swollen nipple and then the other, teased the underside of her nipples before swirling my tongue all around and over them. 'Yes, yes, Mr Cathcart, I'm fine. You said that you wanted me to come up with a spot for the six o'clock news. I can do that.'

He babbled on, and I latched my mouth onto one of Vicky's engorged nipples and sucked on it, pulled on it, tried to swallow up as much of her succulent tit as I could. She bit her lip and thrust out her chest, urging me to devour her breasts. I disgorged her left tit and went to work on her right, clutching and squeezing the sopping flesh of one breast while I nursed on the other. She flipped the phone receiver upside down and moaned, her eyes closed, her upper body undulating gently as I fed on her tits and nipples, felt up her breasts.

Then I abruptly pulled my head back, gave her glistening tits a final playful squeeze, and slipped my fingers under the elasticised band of her shorts. Her eyes popped open and she vaguely shook her head,

Cathcart's tinny voice filling the room. I nodded slowly and surely, and she smiled, and then brought her legs together and arched her body off the chair so that I could slide her shorts off her hips and down her legs. I took my time, the backs of my fingers stroking her slim, supple legs all the way down.

I pulled her shorts off her bare feet, threw them aside, and gazed with delight at her moist pussy. Her clean-shaven mound glistened under the fluorescent lights, her puffy, pink lips crying out to me to tongue and taste her; fuck her with my tongue; lick and suck her clit. She spread her bronzed legs as wide as the chair allowed, and I picked them up and placed them on my shoulders, brought my face to within inches of her pussy.

'Do it!' she hissed, prompting another agitated inquiry from her phone-bound client.

I stared at her pussy for a good, long moment and licked my lips, inhaled the musky scent of her aroused womanhood. Then I ran my tongue down the side of one of her thighs and bit into the vulnerable flesh right next to her pussy. I did the same with her other thigh. She gasped, and her legs quivered as I stroked her inner thighs with my tongue, painted her skin with my saliva.

She covered the phone with her hand and yelled, 'Eat me!', her blue-fire eyes blazing.

I took firm hold of her thighs and plunged my hardened tongue in between her shiny lips, directly into her pussy. Her body jumped, but I held on tight, driving my long tongue deep into her sexual core. Then I started rhythmically fucking her with my tongue.

'Yes!' she shrieked.

I moved my head back and forth, pumping my tongue in and out of her soaking sex, immersing myself in the erotic taste and smell of her pussy. I reached in and spread her slick folds, exposing an even deeper pinkness, and I dragged my tongue in long, hard, slow strokes from her asshole to her clit, over and over.

She held onto the phone for dear life, her face a grim mask of sexual agony. But she still managed to boldly uncover the receiver and say in a strained voice, 'And do you have … any more ideas, Mr Cathcart?' Which, of course, he did.

She was daring me to bring her off while she conducted business as usual on the telephone. I lapped at her pussy repeatedly, savouring the slick feel and tart taste of her drenched cunny. Then I gave her pussy one final lick, smacked my lips with satisfaction, and exposed her clit with my fingers before quickly covering it with my mouth. I sucked hard on her inflamed clitoris, desperate now to bring her to orgasm and drown myself in her honey, my head swimming with the awesome sensuality of it all. She stared fixedly ahead, her teeth clenched, her free hand squeezing her breast, pulling her nipple. I unmouthed her clit only long enough to slap it with my tongue a couple of times, and then I went right back to sucking on it.

'I … I agree, Mr Cathcart,' she gulped into the phone, then yelped when I shoved two fingers into her slit.

That did it. She suddenly went rigid, her muscles locking and standing out in stark relief on her bowed body, and then she was jolted by an orgasm. I ploughed my fingers in and out of her, sucked and tongued her clit, as her sweat-slick body jerked up and down, wave after wave of ecstasy breaking deep inside her. How she managed to stop from screaming – from giving Cathcart a blistering earful of genuine hardcore phone-sex – I have no idea. But she did. She embraced her orally induced orgasms in stunning silence, her rippling body and gushing pussy speaking volumes.

When I returned to work after my vacation; when I was up to my ears in paperwork during the afternoon of my first day back at the office, I received an unexpected visitor.

'Your wife is here to see you,' the receptionist informed me when I picked up the phone.

I hurried out to the reception area, less than happy to be interrupted in the middle of a busy catch-up day. Vicky had been to the office a couple of times in the past, but I actively discouraged her from making any unnecessary pop-in visits; I like to keep my home and business life as separate as possible.

'Hi, sweetheart,' she greeted me when I rounded the corner.

'H-hi,' I stammered, my eyes widening as I took in the outfit she was wearing. She was barely clothed in a white tube-top that fully revealed her flat, brown stomach and diamond-studded bellybutton, and a cherry red mini-skirt that showed off all of her legs and some of her ass. I exchanged glances with the smiling receptionist, then asked, 'Uh, what's up, Vicky?'

'I need you … right away,' she replied coyly.

I hustled her down the hall and into my office

before any more of my co-workers could get an eyeful. 'I'm kind of backed up right now,' I began, before the telephone rang and cut me off. I shut the door, walked past Vicky and scooped up the phone. It was Takkinen from engineering; he wanted to discuss the latest month-end variance report. I gave Vicky a tight smile and gestured for her to sit down.

She didn't. She flipped the lock on the door and then sauntered over and closed the blinds on the window, her tight buns twitching suggestively under that incredibly brief skirt. And while Takkinen nattered away about the four-tonne increase in sulphur usage over year-to-date average, Vicky nonchalantly pulled off her top and unhooked her skirt. She stood before me, in my office, completely and utterly naked save for her sexy, black stilettos.

'Time for some payback,' she stated, grinning evilly.

I eyed her mouth-watering body, my eyes lingering hazardously on her pert tits, her erect nipples, her shining pussy. I tried to make sense out of what Takkinen was telling me, but my brain had gone all warm and mushy when I'd realised what Vicky was up to. She puckered her glossy lips and blew me a kiss, cupped her breasts and spread her long legs apart. She squeezed her tits, rolled her nipples between her fingers, her trim lower body swaying from side to side. Then she turned around and bent at the waist and pointed her round ass at me.

'Yeah, baby,' I murmured, rubbing the hard outline of my cock through my pants.

'What did you call me?' Takkinen asked.

'Huh? Nothing. Just agreeing with you, that's all.

Keep talking.'

Vicky nodded her head, turned to face me again and arched her back and riffled her fingers through her shimmering hair, her hot body searing my eyes as Takkinen talked shop in my ear. She strutted over to me, until we were mere inches apart, whereupon she brushed my hand away from my swollen cock and replaced it with hers.

'I'm going to suck your dick till you come in my mouth,' she breathed into my face.

I nodded excitedly as Takkinen asked if there was someone in the office with me.

'N-no, no,' I said, choking on my wicked lie. 'It was–' I had to halt my explanation and hold my breath when Vicky swiftly unzipped my pants and pulled out my cock, held the rock-hard member in her hot, little hand and squeezed. She glided her hand up and down my engorged manhood, and I swallowed hard and croaked into the phone, 'What's, um, up with that electrical overage? I bet you want to talk about that.'

Takkinen cooperated, went off on a long-winded, technical explanation as Vicky squatted down in front of me and licked at my balls. I groaned, barely able to maintain my composure. She tickled my furry balls with her devilish tongue, her hand swirling all over my stiff cock, and then she sucked one of my balls into her mouth and tugged on it.

I leaned back against the desk and closed my eyes, Takkinen's voice rattling on like a distant train, my wife taking my entire sack in her mouth and pulling on it, juggling my balls with her tongue. She'd had lots of experience with oral sex, and she knew exactly what to do to drive me wild, to rapidly drive me to the brink of orgasm.

I opened my eyes and stared down into Vicky's sky-blue eyes, watched as she sucked and tongued my testicles a while longer, and then disgorged the sopping wet sack and ran her tongue all the way up from my balls to my cockhead, bathing my shaft in warm saliva. She gripped my dick at the base and licked my pulsating cock like she was determinedly tonguing a popsicle before it melted all over her hand.

'Finish me,' I implored, my voice a strangled whisper, my balls boiling with semen.

'If you look at page forty two, line four …' Takkinen continued, not suspecting for a moment that I was getting a wicked blowjob from my gorgeous wife while he was talking to me on the phone.

Vicky tilted my rigid cock downwards and engulfed my dickhead with her mouth, sucked vigorously on the mushroomed cock-top, her tongue buffing the sensitive underside of my hood. Her head bobbed up and down, and she took more and more of my throbbing member into her mouth each time. She could easily swallow all of my cock I well knew – practice makes perfect, after all – but I didn't allow her to get that far this time around. The whole dangerous liaison had inflamed my passions so greatly that I lost control much quicker than usual; so much so that when she had vacuumed up a good three-quarters of my cock, I threw back my head and grunted with joy and rocketed semen into her mouth, down her throat. I clung to her head with one hand, crushed the phone with the other, my body spasming uncontrollably with each and every cum-blast.

Vicky never let up on my rupturing cock, staring up

at me as her throat worked and she swallowed my spurting semen. Takkinen went on and on, but unfortunately I wasn't so lucky; my cock was soon empty, drained of an incredible load by my talented wife. She pulled my spent dick out of her mouth, squeezed a final few drops from my slit and tongued them up. Then she got to her feet, kissed me warmly on the lips, and put her clothes back on.

'Don't waste the whole day yakking on the phone, honey,' she said over her shoulder, as she slipped out the door. 'I know how tiring that can be.'

'You understand what I'm saying?' Takkinen inquired on the other end of the line.

'Sure … sure,' I replied exhaustedly, zipping myself back up with a shaky hand. 'You've been a real help.'

Arlene
by N. Vasco

ARLENE SAT NAKED ON a Persian rug after finishing her yoga, a sheen on her pearly skin, the dim, rosy light from the scented candles illuminating the posh suite her husband reserved for them.

'I'll never get tired of watching you do yoga, baby,' she remembered Mark saying, recalling his almost rapt expression when he watched her.

'He's such an idiot.' she playfully thought, while extending her legs, pointing her toes and admiring the red polish on her toenails; the slender gold chains around her ankles and the little rings on her toes reflecting the candlelight.

Her bare skin still tingled in the cool air. Her nipples itched nicely. When she began caressing her feet she felt horny and wanted to masturbate.

'But I don't have the time,' she thought while laying back, raising her legs straight into the air, pointing her toes and grasping her ankles, admiring the shadows playing in the sexy definitions of her legs. She pulled feet back and tucked them behind her head, enjoying the deliciously sexy stretch in her calves and hamstrings. It was such a struggle to keep her body in shape after their third child but yoga and steady visits to the gym helped a lot. She always thought her breasts were too small, her hips too wide and her ass too big. For some insane reason, Mark never ceased praising her body.

'It wasn't just that incredible ass, babe,' she remembered him saying as she caressed the stretched curve of her buttock, her pulse rising under her pearly skin. 'Or those wicked, exotic eyes, or those incredible hips. It's your sexy femininity that made my cock as hard as a rock when I first saw you.'

'He's such an asshole,' she said, while smiling and cupping her pliant yet firm cheeks, her nails digging into them, electricity rippling under her skin as she recalled how they made love last night. She strutted into the bedroom in a red, hi-cut thong teddy and stiletto healed sandals – the straps around her ankles – leaned against the dresser and arched her bottom out.

Before she knew it Mark was kneeling behind her and thrusting that excellent tongue deep inside her while cupping and squeezing her buttocks, thighs and hips as that wonderfully familiar, juicy surge of ecstasy seized her body.

The orgasm came quickly. Too quickly. She wanted to feel him hard and firm insider her but indulged him when he insisted he on feasting on her some more.

Lying on the bed, she enjoyed his hands caressing her body before he slowly undid the straps around her ankles, his tongue teasing her feet. When he finished removing her heels, he licked and sucked her pointed toe as she throbbed and ached for his cock until she demanded he fuck her. When he delayed, she pushed him down on the bed, mounted his hard, veined manhood and rode vigorously.

'Don't you dare tease me like that, you beautiful son of a bitch!' She remembered almost shouting, not caring if the kids heard her. She enjoyed him like that until she slid off, crouched on all fours, raised her bottom and told him to give it to her 'hard and deep,' Mark gladly obliging and thrusting so deep she let out a gasping cry into her pillow.

'Yes! Yes!' she remembered moaning and when he raised one foot on the bed so he could go deeper, his hands grabbing her hips, drawing her closer, her second orgasm came in a rush that shattered her soul into thousands of glistening shards.

By now, Arlene felt that pleasant wet sensation in her crotch and slid an elegant finger inside her wet love.

'Better stop now,' she said while unhooking her feet from behind her head, standing up and, after blowing the candles out and turning on the lights, looking at the package on the bed for her.

Mark had taken care of everything. Hotel reservations, dinner at the five-star restaurant on the first floor, the kids at her mother's. She wondered if Jeremy had his allergy medicine, or if Christine's science project was due next week, and was Mark's football game this Saturday?

'Stop it!' she told herself while sitting on the bed. 'This is our night and nothing's getting in the way. Not the kids, the tyres on the mini-van, nor that witch Carla in accounting and the bids for the new PCs we have to buy.'

All thoughts of kids, work and anything else melted away when she opened the package, her eyes catching the short, fitted blue cocktail dress, little blue lace thong and blue mules, the heels and toe box wickedly pointed.

'Must be a night for the colour blue,' she thought after slipping on the dress, the silky fabric feeling so nice against her skin, her erect nipples nicely visible on the delicate weave, the thong now nested so nicely between her cheeks.

It took a few moments to get used to the heels.

'Impractical, completely and utterly useless except for one thing,' she muttered to herself while walking around and getting used to them.

'Only a couple of hours, after that, they come off, one way or another!'

She stopped in front on the mirror, admiring the sexy definition of her calves and thighs and the way her buttocks seemed to arch out even more, the sight of her body reminding her how horny she felt.

'Okay, maybe more than a couple of hours. I bet I'll be off my feet one way or another anyway.'

She glanced at the package, saw a small blue envelope and after opening it, pulled out a familiar looking black velvet choker, reminding her of the sexy game they sometimes played. Whenever she wore it she could do anything she wanted. He was her love slave and there was nothing he could refuse; oral sex in a public place (parking lots and mini-vans are so handy); a quickie at his job (in the cupboard) or licking her anus when they were in the shower.

The choker reminded her of how she figured out a way to satisfy the typical male fantasy of watching two women. It was Mark's birthday and to celebrate she hired one of those sexy internet models, not expecting the evening to get as hot as it did until Penny, the long-legged model she hired, showed up at the door, looking so sexy in a little leather skirt and tight top. Arlene experienced her fair share of experimenting in college and knew how much fun a woman could be, and while she and Mark had talked about a threesome the thought of letting a third person into their relationship just didn't seem right.

'Until that night with Penny,' Arlene thought while clasping the choker around her neck. The 'photo session' started with her and Penny wearing only black, sheer gowns and posing by the fireplace or the black leather sofa in the living room, and wound up getting really hot when she asked Penny if she wouldn't mind posing nude.

Penny replied by letting the gown pool around her pretty feet before helping Arlene out of hers, and before she knew it, they were groping each other's bodies, their thighs wrapped around each other as they shared a deep, tongue-probing kiss; Mark all the while taking picture after picture.

They wound up in a scissors position, their crotches grinding against each other. When they lay back and rubbed each other's breasts and erect nipples with their feet, she felt her orgasm seize her body, making her writhe and groan, her loud moans joining Penny's as she came too.

The evening wasn't over after she and Penny got dressed. She knew Mark was horny when he joined them by the front door, the gym shorts he wore doing nothing to hide his throbbing erection, making her and Penny giggle like a couple of schoolgirls. When Mark asked what was so funny, Arlene responded by kneeling and pulling down his shorts before taking the entire length of his hot, hard meat in her mouth, Penny cheering her on.

She sucked and gulped loudly for a while, teasing and caressing his nipples and when she nodded at Penny, she slipped his cock out of her mouth, grabbed Penny's hips and backed that sexy, tight ass against her husband's cock. She didn't give Mark a chance to react as she hitched up Penny's little skirt and slipped his pole inside her wet pussy, her moans and sighing gasps filling the room. When she saw Mark hesitating, she looked him in the eye while fingering the choker around her neck.

'Remember baby,' she said. 'You have to do everything I tell you. And right now, I want you to be a good host and give our pretty little guest a good fuck.'

With that she knelt in front of Penny while reaching back, clutching Marks sexy ass and pulling his cock even deeper while licking Penny's exposed clit and drenched crotch. Mark gladly obliged as Arlene savoured Penny's flowing juices, their combined moans getting louder until she felt them both heave and shudder, Arlene still feasting away on Penny.

They traded a final kiss at the door until Arlene asked Mark to excuse them and, after he left, she wrapped her arm's around Penny's sexy body and looked into her lovely brown doe eyes.

'I like you Penny. And this was fun. But if you ever get between me and my husband, I'll kill you.'

They shared a good laugh after that, Penny reassuring her she would never sink that low, despite not having a steady lover for over a year.

'Yeah, I can enjoy a hook-up whenever I want. It's

just so hard finding the right person to be there for you. Or you for them.'

She still traded e-mails with Penny on occasion and chatted on the phone once in a while.

'A sweet girl, too bad she can't find the right guy, or girl.'

She left the room, took the lift to the lobby and remembered the first time she and Mark had anal sex; how gentle and patient he was and how such a wicked combination of pain and pleasure could feel so good.

She stepped out of the elevator and walked across the lobby to the lounge, registering the stares from the bellboys and the woman at the concierge desk; they probably thought she was a hooker on the prowl, or some freak looking to rock someone's world.

'I'm a little bit of both,' she thought while heading for the restaurant. When she stepped into the somewhat crowded happy-hour, most of the servers, busboys and patrons immediately took notice of her as her phone rang.

'You look incredible,' she heard Mark say as she scanned the room, avoiding every longing, inviting look trying to grab her attention.

'Where are you?' she asked.

'Just direct that sweet, sexy stride of yours up to the bar,' he replied. 'I'll be with you shortly.'

He hung up as she made her way to an empty part of the bar and sat down, glad that the stool's high back offered a little bit of cover as she crossed her legs and ordered a drink. Her phone rang again.

'Look behind you. I'm in the crowd.'

When she looked over her shoulder she could see people here and there chatting at their tables, eating and enjoying themselves, but no Mark.

'Where are you?' she said. That's when her eyes caught a very handsome, broad-shouldered man in a sports coat, tight polo-shirt and fitted slacks looking at her. His eyes were hazel and he wore his long blond hair in a ponytail.

It wasn't Mark.

'I'm over here.'

A hand rested on her bare shoulder. The fingers were long but solid, the palm callused and strong and when she looked at those beautiful brown eyes she felt like making love right there on the bar. He wore the suit she always liked on him, but before she could plant a long, tongue-probing kiss on those sexy lips he gestured over her shoulder and introduced Phil, his college buddy.

It was the handsome blond guy with the ponytail.

The night seemed to melt into one long, pleasant evening of jokes, drinks, good food and very good company. The three of them sat in a booth right up until midnight and as the time flew by, Arlene had never felt so horny in her entire life. She loved the way Mark held her hand and the occasional feeling of Phil's muscular thigh when he made a joke or moved to get a drink and, when he excused himself for a moment, she threw Mark a questioning look.

'You can take off the choker right now,' he said while holding her hand in his and gazing into her eyes. 'Or,' he said, while gently running a finger across her cheek and sending shivers of anticipation through her body, 'you can keep it on.'

When his friend returned, Mark told her Phil was a licensed masseur and worked his way through college giving massages.

'It was an ordeal, believe it or not,' Phil said with that sexy, Australian accent. 'Zits, back hair, sweat. And then there were the blokes!'

'Believe it or not,' Mark said before raising her hand and giving it a tender kiss, 'this incredibly hot, sexy woman a loser like me was privileged to marry occasionally suffers from lower back aches.'

'When he says loser, he's right,' Phil emphasised with that sexy voice, those golden-coloured eyebrows arched. 'You should have seen the women he dated. Or better yet, not. Scare a dingo out of its den.'

Before Arlene knew it, the three of them were back in the suite. She lay on a massage table that had conveniently appeared in living room, naked except for the choker and little towel covering her buttocks, while enjoying Mark's hands on her feet as Phil massaged her lower back, his hands just above the swell of her buttocks. Both of them had doffed their jackets and shirts.

It was heaven.

Two pairs of excellent, masculine hands kneading and stroking her legs back and thighs, washing her body with ripples of pleasure, her pussy a well of wet, aching passion that yearned to be pleased. It was then she felt another set of hands take her other foot and begin massaging it as she felt Mark's tongue lick and tease her feet and before long, Phil began doing the same.

Then, she felt the towel slip off her buttocks just before someone gently parted her thighs and lavished her drenched crotch with a hot, probing tongue, making her let out a gasping moan that caught her by surprise.

Everything turned into a blur of erotic release. She closed her eyes as she felt another set of lips, so masculine, so wonderfully unfamiliar, feast away at her crotch as Mark's stiff, solidly veined meat slipped into her mouth. She sucked hard as Phil tongued and probed her pussy, her hot breaths gasping for air, making her feel like the luckiest woman in the world. Sure the PTA hags would ridicule her if they found out. Sure her boss would be shocked and that bitch Carol would be green with envy right now in her dark little cubicle as she poured over her paperwork.

She didn't care. Instead, she took Mark's wonderful cock in her mouth while reaching back and guiding Phil's veined manhood inside the yielding walls of her pussy, that hard-yet-soft, delicious sensation filling her to the brim before it began to slide in and out of her body.

She loved it. When they traded places, Mark's shaft filling her pussy, she relished it as much as the taste of her juices coating Phil's cock. She sucked away eagerly, taking him as deep as her throat allowed, her ears catching Mark's sexy grunts as he pumped away.

Suddenly, the most wicked thought she ever had entered her mind.

Sometimes, when they had anal sex, she would slide a small vibrator inside her pussy. It always got the both of them off and the conversations they would have afterward, of her enjoying the thought of two rigid cocks inside her, would make them wind up making love again shortly afterwards.

After a few words and gestures, she found herself on the bed, on top of Mark, her back to him while guiding that deliciously hard pole inside her anus and gesturing Phil to slide his rigid cock inside her aching pussy.

As she gasped and moaned, she realised how familiar it felt, yet how new it all seemed. That overwhelming sensation of her body filled by these handsome studs

The pleasure she had been nursing all night turned into a flood of erotic, mind- shattering passion that sent her into one of the most intense orgasms of her life just before Mark and Phil came at the same time and filled her up with their hot juices.

When it was over she rolled on her side, Mark's spent cock still inside her as she wrapped a thigh around Phil's waist, just enjoying the afterglow until excusing herself and stepping into the bathroom, avoiding any awkward or clumsy words that could ruin the moment.

She freshened up, put on the short, black silk robe Mark had gotten her last Valentine's day, and, after checking her make-up, she stopped in front of the full-length mirror in front of the door and admired herself one last time. Again she admired her feet, one ankle slightly raised, her gaze wandering up the creamy expanse of her legs, the hem of the robe barely covering her crotch, the silky material clinging to her hips. She caressed her bare thighs as her gaze rested on her face.

'Still the same person, no matter what.'

When she stepped into the living room she saw to her surprise Phil, now fully dressed, his sport coat over his shoulder, standing by the door.

'Mark just wanted me to have the chance to say

good-bye,' he said, extending his hand. She took it, savouring the strong yet gentle quality of his grip as he looked at her for one last time with those lovely blue eyes.

'I was only joking about him being a loser,' Phil told her. 'With a woman like you he's a winner. I only hope I find someone like you one day.

It was then she remembered Penny and decided Phil would be a perfect match.

'I'm sure you will. As a matter of fact, you can bet on it.'

Before giving him a chance to reply, she kissed his cheek, promised they'd stay in touch, closed the door and leaned against it, savouring the memory of what had happened only moments ago, her fingers eventually wandering up to the choker.

Then, with a wicked grin on her face, she turned to the bedroom door, knowing Mark was waiting for her.

'If he thinks the night is over, he's got another thing coming.'

Sauntering to the bedroom, she laughed at such a bad pun, knowing the night had just begun.

The Boss
by Ruby Latour

JADE WATCHED HIM. IT wasn't as if she had never seen him before. She had known him for months now; they worked in the same company after all. He had always been quite friendly, but she was wary of him. He had a reputation. He always had a different woman, women seemed to love him, and she hadn't really seen what the attraction was. His name was John; an average name for an average guy. He was fairly tall, quite attractive but nothing outstanding.

He looked over at her and Jade quickly looked away, embarrassed that he may have seen her watching him. When she looked back their eyes met and he smiled; he had seen her. Jade wanted to turn away again but for some reason couldn't bring herself to do so. He left the crowd of beautiful girls that surrounded him and made his way over to her.

She felt herself frozen to the spot, unable to move and not sure even if she wanted to.

'Hi,' he said, staring right into her eyes now.

'Hi,' she replied, wishing she could think of something to say.

'You look great tonight,' he leant in close as he said

it, and as he drew away his eyes moved up and down her body obviously appreciating what he saw.

She was glad she had made an effort now. Her long dark hair hung in loose curls down her back and her black strappy dress clung to her every curve.

'You don't look so bad yourself,' Jade replied, and regretted it the moment she said it. He did look good, effortlessly good. A simple black shirt and well cut black trousers that complimented his lean body.

'So, are you having fun?' he asked, standing much closer than necessary. Jade was beginning to feel hot.

'Yeah, it's a good party,' she was lying now; it wasn't a good party; it was a typical company event; boring and stuffy. She was only there because her boss had insisted.

'I think you're lying, Jade,' he whispered in her ear. 'You think it's boring, just like I do.'

She laughed; he had read her mind.

'John, this is dull, how about we go on somewhere else?' They had been joined by two of the girls he had been talking to earlier. They were even more beautiful close up and Jade felt dowdy in comparison.

'No, I don't think so, I'm staying here,' he smiled at them, his hand gently touching Jade's lower back as he did so. They looked disappointed and tried to convince him to change his mind but eventually gave up and left.

'Why didn't you go with them?' Jade asked, as they made their exit. She was bemused, they were stunning, very drunk and obviously up for a very good time.

'Because I want to spend the night with you.' His eyes bored into hers; she knew he meant the night and not just the evening.

'Is that right?' She smiled at him, sounding far more confident than she felt. She couldn't believe how sexy he was, how had she never noticed it before.

'Oh yes, Jade, that's right,' he was teasing her now. 'I'm going to play with your pussy all night, let's get some more drinks.' He gently led her to the bar. She said nothing. She was shocked; she was surprised, but she couldn't drag herself away.

'I can't believe you just said that,' she said finally, when he handed her another glass of wine.

'Can't you, why, don't you want me to?' His face was serious now and only inches away from hers.

'I don't know.' Jade felt breathless.

'I think you do know Jade.' She loved the way he said her name 'So tell me.'

'Yes,' she said quietly taking a gulp of her drink.

'Yes what?'

'Yes I want you to.'

'You want me to what? I want to hear you say it Jade.'

'I want you to play with me,' she whispered in his ear, not quite believing what she was doing.

'Mmm that's better, do you want me to play with you here?' He edged closer to her.

'No!' Jade spat. He was outrageous, she loved it.

'So do you want me to take you back to my place and play with you?' His fingers brushed the side of her thigh.

'Yes,' she sighed, desperate to leave the party and be alone with him. He smiled a wide sexy smile; he had got the answer he wanted.

Neither of them said much in the taxi; they had said

enough. Jade thought he might try to kiss her or touch her but he didn't. When they arrived at his flat after ten minutes of small talk in the car, Jade almost thought she had imagined their conversation earlier. She hadn't.

He poured two glasses of wine and stood looking at her as they both drank. The minutes felt like hours and she was desperate for him to touch her. He knew it. Then slowly he put both wine glasses down and ran his fingers over the thin straps of her dress. He kissed her, slowly, gently at first but then his tongue was deep inside her mouth and she felt him undo the zip on the back of her dress. He eased the dress down and it fell to the floor, while all the time his tongue probed in and out of her mouth. Jade felt her bra being removed with the same expertise and he slowly moved away from her, standing back to admire what he had just unwrapped.

He smiled, liking what he saw. Jade felt vulnerable standing with her dress around her feet and only wearing a small pair of sheer black knickers. He stood so that he was behind her; he kissed her neck and his left hand played with her left nipple, flicking it backwards and forward; making it hard.

'Your tits are amazing, I can't wait to suck them.' Jade shivered and John slid his hand into her knickers. Slowly he edged his fingers down between her legs. He rubbed himself up against her back and she could feel how hard he was.

'God, your pussy is so wet, I can't wait to eat you,' he murmured into her neck as he gently played with her 'I think I better get you into the bedroom quick.'

He moved away suddenly removing his hand. Jade sighed, desperately wanting more.

He pushed her onto the bed and stood beside it, undressing as he looked at her.

'I think we better take these off now, don't you? They're soaking!' He smiled as he roughly removed her knickers. Jade opened her legs wide for him and he needed no invitation. He sucked her nipples hard, first one and then the other, with one finger, then two, inside her. Jade moaned, loving what he was doing.

She reached for his cock; it was huge. Her hand tightened around him; she wanted to make him feel as good as he was making her. He pulled away; she looked surprised.

'Don't worry, Jade, there will plenty of time for that later.' He moved down her body. 'I've just got to lick your cunt right now.' The tip of his tongue traced up and down her thighs; she knew he was teasing her and she couldn't bear it. Around and around he licked her but not moving towards the desired spot. When she could take it no longer she cried, 'John, please.' As if right on cue, his tongue entered her; slowly; quickly; he knew what he was doing. His hands gripped either side of her waist as he made her wetter and wetter with every move of his tongue.

'Yes! Yes!' She writhed around knowing that he would soon make her come 'More, more!'

He stopped suddenly and before Jade could protest he lay beside her. 'Sit on my face, I can't get deep enough inside your pussy.'

'But I was about to come,' she sighed.

'You'll come better on top of me, I want to lick your clit properly.'

She did as she was told and was glad that she did. Within seconds John was doing things to her cunt she didn't know were possible.

'I'm going to come, I'm going to come on your face,' she cried, as the sensation swept over her body. She rubbed her cunt backwards and forwards over his mouth. She felt herself orgasm as John continued to lick her out.

Her body was still shuddering as she felt John slide out from underneath her and sit behind her. His finger took over from where his tongue had been and she was still coming as he started to play with her again.

'Oh my God, I'm still coming,' she cried, bearing down on his hand as his cock rubbed in between her legs from behind.

'And you're going to keep on coming,' he said, knowing exactly what he was doing to her.

He was incredible; his left hand was bouncing her tits up and down while his right hand was finger-fucking her and making her wetter than she had ever been before in her life; the tip of his dick was edging to take over from where his fingers were inside her.

'Fuck me,' she moaned.

'Don't worry, I'm going to,' he laughed.

'Fuck me now, I'm so wet for you'

'I'm going to make you come again first.' He kissed her neck.

Jade's hand reached between her legs for his cock.

'Your cock is huge –I want to feel you inside me.'

'You've got to come for me first.' His fingers moved quicker and quicker.

He pinched her nipples hard and thrust two fingers deep inside her.

'Oh my God, that's it,' she cried, 'I'm going to come again.'

'I know baby, I know. And then I'm going to fuck you.'

'Tell me,' she cried. 'Tell me.'

'When you come, I'm going to put my cock inside your beautiful cunt and fuck you so hard, you dirty bitch.'

'Oh my God, more, more!' Jade moaned, loving him talking dirty to her.

'I'm going to be so deep inside you, in-and-out, in-and-out, and you're going to come with me fucking you.'

'Yes, yes!

'I'm going to shoot my load deep inside your pussy.'

'Yeah, faster, John, flick my clit, baby.'

'Are you going to come for me Jade?'

'Yes.'

'And then are you going to let me fuck you?'

'Yes.'

'Good girl.' His fingers got what they wanted and Jade came even harder than the first time.

'That's amazing yes, yes,' she cried as she came and just when she thought it couldn't get any better John entered her from behind.

'I want to feel to you come around my cock.' He thrust in and out of her, his balls banging against her arse.

'Oh yes, harder.'

'Say it, Jade.'

'Fuck me, fuck me harder.'

She was on all fours, her tits swinging as he pushed

in and out.

'Fuck, your tits are incredible; can you feel how hard I am for you?'

'Yeah, oh yeah,' she opened her legs wider for him.

'You feel amazing.' It was his turn to groan now, she was loving it.

'How amazing?' She was teasing him.

'Your cunt is so tight around my cock; you're so wet I'm slipping in and out of you. Turn over.'

She lay on her back and he pushed her legs back towards her head.

This time when he entered her it was deeper; she could feel the whole length of him inside her.

He put her legs over his shoulders and went deeper still. Again and again, getting faster and faster, Jade couldn't believe that she was going to come again.

'Oh yeah, more, harder,' she heard herself cry.

'Is that good?' he asked.

'Yes, yes, you are so deep – fuck, you're so big – I'm going to come.'

'Me too, I'm going to fill your cunt up,' he smiled, looking into her eyes, ramming himself into her again and again.

As she came she tightened around his rock-hard cock and he shuddered inside her, climaxing at the same time. Jade seemed to come over and over again, she had never known anything like it.

They lay side by side, catching their breath.

'You are a great fuck, that was amazing,' John finally said.

'So I take it you're pleased you made me come to the party then?' Jade smiled up at him.

'Now you know why I did.' He looked pleased with

himself.

'Well you know me; I would never say no to the boss, would I?'

'I'm very glad to hear it Jade, now come here, I've got another little job for you …'

Company Picnic
by Chloe Devlin

GRETA APPROACHED THE GROUP in the park with more than a little apprehension. As a temp, she didn't quite feel she belonged at the company picnic. But Marcus and Dominic had insisted she show up. Since they were the top salesman and respected by everyone, she found herself in a position where she couldn't refuse. Even so, she hadn't worn the spike heels that Marcus had ordered her to wear. That sort of attire would've been completely inappropriate at this kind of affair.

Laughter burst from the middle of a knot of people, reminding her she wasn't truly a part of this group, this company.

Just as she turned to leave, a hand grasped her upper arm. 'Where do you think you're going?' a voice murmured in her ear.

She looked up into Marcus' smiling face. 'I was just … um, I mean …'

He slid his arm around her shoulders, squeezing her against his side. 'Don't tell me you were thinking of leaving? Dom and I would be heartbroken. We've been looking forward to eating … with you.'

She drew in a deep breath, the musky scent of

Marcus mingling with the clean smell of freshly cut grass. As his fingertips rubbed gently against her bare arm, she felt a sudden surge of arousal deep in her belly. Why here? Why now? she thought. After all these years of nothing.

Happier than she would've imagined being that she had come to this picnic, she smiled. 'Well, we wouldn't want you or Dominic to be heartbroken. Lead on.'

'Good girl.'

The praise warmed her cheeks, sending spirals of lust even deeper. She let Marcus draw her into the close group of picnickers. After a brief wave of greeting, she settled back against his sun-warmed body, content to listen to the conversation as it flowed around her. She caught snippets here and there.

'– and the whole floor heard Parson's wife screaming at him that she wanted a divorce because he was a lying, cheating bastard who –'

'I don't know what more I can do. His letters are already done in record time, everything is filed properly. And I even arrange for refills of his prescriptions, including his "little blue pill."'

'Heard a rumour that the company is going public. Anyone with stock options is going to be a happy camper.'

'But yesterday, he called me into his office to look at this tiny rock. He wanted me to guess what it was. Looks like a tiny rock to me, I said. You know what it was? A kidney stone! *His* kidney stone! I so did not need to see his kidney stone.'

Greta's attention got pulled away from the different conversations that were tumbling over each other when

Marcus began tracing patterns on her thigh with his fingertip. Even though the material of her sundress, she could feel the heat from his hand and the firmness of his fingers against her. She sucked in a breath as the tracings wandered farther up her leg, nearly sliding in between her inner thighs. Much closer to her crotch and he'd be able to feel the warmth that dampened her panties.

Before she could reach down and discreetly remove his wandering fingers, he lifted them from her leg. Then he tucked a strand of hair behind her ear as he nuzzled her lobe. 'I hope you're getting hungry,' he murmured, then swirled his tongue in her ear, sending a shudder through her body. 'Dom and I are starving … for you.'

Another tiny spurt of moisture dampened her panties even more. She wondered if anyone else could smell her arousal. Much more of this touching and nibbling and her entire body would go up in flames. After these few caresses, she was hotter than she could ever remember being, especially in the past several years.

'Oh, food's ready!' One of the secretaries interrupted her thoughts, pointing toward the table next to the grill. A basket piled high with hamburger and hot dog buns sat next to a platter filled with burgers, dogs and even a chicken breast or two. A huge tub of coleslaw sat next to an equally large tub of potato salad.

As the group stood and moved towards the food, Greta allowed herself to be guided by Marcus. He kept one hand resting on the small of her back, possessive in a gentle manner. Another hand on her waist startled her. When she looked up, Dominic stood at her other side, his touch equally possessive. Yet she didn't feel like the bone between two growling dogs, but rather like a root beer float shared between two lovers.

'You smell delightful,' Dom said. 'Like a burst of freshness.'

She raised an eyebrow. 'What does a "burst of freshness" smell like?'

He sniffed her hair. 'I don't know. But you do.' Leaning down, he whispered in her ear. 'And it's making me incredibly hard. Wanna feel?'

Greta swallowed, suddenly aware that she was practically sandwiched between two tall, strong, aroused males. Yet looking around, she knew that no one was paying any attention to the three of them as they moved through the food line.

Once she had her plate, she watched Dom and Marcus as they casually strolled towards the woods. No words were spoken, but instinctively she knew they wanted her to follow. And she wanted to follow them and discover more of the sensual magic they were weaving.

After they had gone several hundred yards into the forested area of the park, the two men veered off the main path, cutting around several large tree trunks before coming to a small clearing. In the middle of the leaf-strewn area, two light blue blankets sat on an old-fashioned picnic table. And on top of the blankets, white rope lay coiled like a waiting snake.

She stopped between two trees, holding her plate of food that contained one burger on half of a bun and a small serving of coleslaw. In her other hand, her fingers curved around a cold drink, rivulets of perspiration running down the sides of the can onto her hand.

After placing his food on one end of the table, Marcus set the coil of rope to one side on the edge of one of the benches. Then he flared open one of the blankets, letting it float down and cover the rough wood of the table. 'Come, Greta. Have a seat.'

A zillion thoughts raced through her mind, but none of them made much sense. Except for one. Here was her chance to live out one of her fantasies. One of those deep, dark, intense fantasies that she stuffed way down underneath her everyday life. The type of fantasies that she could never even mention because her sister would think she was some sort of deviant.

Taking a deep breath, she grabbed her courage along with the fantasy and yanked it out into the open. 'Thanks, Marcus. I appreciate the special care you've taken this evening and I'm looking forward to more from you and Dominic.'

As she sat down across from both men, she saw a look of surprise, then appreciation arc between them. Curving her lips into a slight smile, she began to eat. She hadn't thought she was that hungry or that she'd be able to each much, especially knowing what the two men had in mind for her. But the taste of the food made her ravenous and she quickly finished off all the food on her plate.

Marcus removed their empty plates from the picnic table. 'I like a woman with a good appetite for food. Means she has other healthy appetites.'

'And we like healthy appetites,' Dom interjected. He stood and walked around the table.

'When he touched her shoulder, she looked up at

him, seeing the last rays of sunlight shine against his cheekbones, sliding over his full lips. Lips that were sensuous; lips that she imagined against hers. 'Come with me,' he said. 'We'll let Marcus set everything up.'

Greta glanced at the coil of rope, wondering exactly what the two salesmen had planned for her. She allowed Dominic to lead her into the trees, his arm around her waist, guiding and helping her over a tree root.

'Tell me about your experience,' he commanded. 'How many guys have you been with?'

Even with his guiding hand, she stumbled over a loose branch. 'Um … there've been, well …'

They stopped walking and turned so her back was against the rough bark of a tree. Dominic placed his hands on her shoulders. 'It's important, Greta. Marcus and I need to know so we don't hurt you.' He rubbed his palms up and down her bare arms. 'Well, no more than you want us to.'

'I see.' She kept her voice low and steady, despite the increase in her heartbeat.

Grasping her hands, Dominic drew them above her head. He moved forward, his hard body pressing against hers. She shivered, feeling his hard shaft nudging at her belly.

'So, Greta,' he murmured. 'How many men have you fucked?'

She looked up into his intense dark eyes. 'Dom, I … only three. And it's been a while.'

'How long is "a while"?'

She swallowed; her mouth dry. 'Four years.'

'Four years? That's a long time,' he said. 'Way too

long for a woman as hot as you.'

He shifted his hips, rubbing his cock against her belly. She moaned at the sensation, getting more and more aroused.

'Marcus and I are about to change that.' His lips met hers as he kissed her, his tongue plunging into her mouth. Her knees went weak as heat swept through her body.

'Dom! Everything's ready.' Marcus interrupted the kiss.

When Dom released her mouth, she looked over at Marcus. Marcus stood in front of a large tree, a length of white rope held loosely in his left hand. He beckoned with his other hand. 'Come here and we'll start.'

Dom let her hands go, then led her over to Marcus. He turned her so she faced away from Marcus, then bent his head and kissed her again. As Dom nibbled on her lips, Marcus drew her hands behind her. The rope looped around her wrists, tying them together. Not so tight as to dig into her skin, but there was no way she was going to break loose.

As soon as he finished tying her up, Marcus spun her around to face him. He took her lips in a hard kiss, plunging his tongue deep inside her mouth. Her heart pounded harder, thumping against her chest, then stopped for a second as two hands reached around and cupped her breasts.

She gasped into Marcus' mouth as Dom rolled her nipples between his strong fingers. A groan escaped her as both men thrust their hips against her, creating a sandwich with their cocks pressed against her.

Marcus lifted his mouth and spoke to Dom. 'I think

we need to head back to the table,' he gasped. 'I really need to fuck her now.'

'Fine,' Dom growled next to her ear. 'Lead the way. We'll follow, but I'm not letting go of these nipples.'

Dom marched her back to the clearing, continuing to pinch her buds. His dick nudged the crack between her butt cheeks and it felt absolutely huge to her.

'Ready for dessert?' Dom licked the side of her neck, then sucked the soft skin where it met her collarbone.

She made a soft noise – more of a squeak than anything – but coherent words seemed beyond her capabilities. The two guys took the sound as an assent and set her on the edge of the blanket-covered picnic table.

With swift motions, Dom efficiently stripped her sundress over her head, baring her aching breasts to the cool night air, while Marcus drew her soaking panties off her hips and down her legs.

Marcus knelt and reached for her ankles, spreading her legs apart. She felt her pussy throb in response to his intense stare, a spurt of moisture dripping from her lips. He rested a foot on each bench, then tied them in place.

When he finished securing her ankles, he ran his hands up the insides of her legs until he gripped her inner thighs. Instinctively, she tried to close her legs, but he didn't let her, keeping her bared to his gaze.

Behind her, Dom released her wrists, then tilted her back until she lay on the tabletop. She allowed him to take her hands and tie them down to the table, stretched above her head.

A shiver of excitement ran through her body. This

was turning out to be so much more than she had ever dreamed it could be. How did these guys know exactly what to say and do? Which words would turn her insides to mush? Which actions would set her pussy on fire? 'Um … guys, I …'

'Hush, darling' Dom laid his hand over her mouth. She looked up, staring at his upside-down face, then gave in to the temptation to nip at the soft side where his thumb met his palm. 'Aah! You little witch! Guess it's time to get a little tough with you.'

Oh, yes, please, she wanted to plead. But kept her mouth shut, not daring to say anything that would stop them from acting out the rest of her fantasy. She was afraid that if she begged too hard, they would lose interest and let her go. And she definitely didn't want that. At least, not until she had come so hard, it felt like her eyes were crossing.

'Now that we've all had dinner, it's time for dessert,' Dom said. 'How about a banana split sundae?'

She opened her mouth to reply, but shrieked with pleasure instead as Marcus traced a path through her labia with his tongue. He curled the tip around her clit, then sucked hard on the tiny nub, sending spasms of delight through her body. 'Oh, don't stop,' she pleaded. 'Keep going. I want to come!'

As Marcus continued his oral assault on her pussy and clit, Dom tapped on the corner of her mouth with his cockhead. When had he undressed? Must've been when Marcus started licking her. She opened her mouth, letting him slide the hard shaft through her open lips and over her waiting tongue. Closing her lips around the taut skin, she began sucking as he gently thrust in and out of her mouth.

'That's it, darling. Suck my cock!'

Dom reached down and began to tug on her nipples, stretching them out from her body before pinching them between his fingers. Flames of exquisite ecstasy shot through her body. She'd never realised how sensitive her tits, especially her nipples, were. But she loved the rough treatment that Dom was giving hers.

Everything she felt multiplied when Marcus stopped licking her and shoved his big, hard cock straight into her pussy. She squeezed her muscles around the huge shaft, thrilling to the way he pumped in and out of her.

'Damn, her cunt is tight.' Marcus groaned as he continued to pound into her. 'I'm not gonna last long at all. She's too hot!'

'No problem,' Dom gasped. 'We'll just have to screw her again when we're done. I definitely want a piece of that ass.'

Hearing them talk about fucking her ass, combined with the thought that she was pleasuring two men at once, sent her spiralling out of control. Her body stiffened and she gasped for air around the dick that filled her mouth. The waves of her orgasm crashed over her and her body shuddered and shivered beneath the onslaught. Each sensation built upon the last, forcing her higher and higher until the bubble of pleasure burst.

'That's it, baby,' Marcus said. 'Come for us! And we'll come for you.'

With a muffled cry, she went limp; her brain completed drained of thought, her body satiated beyond belief. Within seconds, both men reached their own orgasms, groaning as their pricks erupting into her body – one in her pussy, the other in her mouth. She squeezed her cunt muscles in rhythm with her throat as she swallowed, to milk as much as she could from the two men.

When all three had finished coming, the men withdrew from her body, but left her tied – legs spread, hands over her head – to the picnic table. They sat next to her, straddling the picnic benches.

Marcus stroked strands of her hair from her glistening face, smoothing them down. 'I hope you're enjoying yourself, baby.'

She looked from one side to the other, searching each man's face for a long moment. 'It's everything I imagined. And more. I just want to lay here for ever with you guys.'

Dom smiled and tweaked her nipple. 'Well, maybe not for ever, but I'd say we've got all night.'

The Journey
by Izzy French

CLICK, CLICK, CLICK. EVA'S heels echoed behind her with increasing frequency as she ran for the train. Like a small boy's cap gun, she thought, also wondering how there was space for that thought to have intruded into her overcrowded mind. Her anxiety was palpable; her hands shook, her teeth were clenched. She had to catch that train. David's reaction at breakfast had been as expected. His egg was hard, his toast cold, his tea weak. He hated her going. Thought it unnecessary. A couple of nights away to visit an aged aunt, who had little, if nothing, now to offer. He always measured people on what they had to offer. And it was her second visit in a month. He resented the hold Aunt Millicent appeared to have over her. Thought she had lived an inappropriate life. Might be a bad influence. As if Eva wasn't a grown woman able to make her own choices. She hummed silently, hoping that she could drown out the sound of his voice, peremptory and bad tempered. And there was no pretence at concern. No, his words and actions made it perfectly clear he hated losing control, even temporarily, over his wife. Didn't think he should have to be bothered with domestic duties, even for a day or so. As she stepped aboard and walked down the carriage she suppressed the desire to speculate about how it would feel to be free of him. Why raise her own hopes?

She made her way to the sleeper carriage. Still physically tense, there'd been a subtle change in her anxiety. It had become more anticipatory. From childhood onwards she'd loved train journeys; found them romantic and exciting. She rubbed her left hand against the wool of her skirt, hoping it would absorb the dampness, not leave a mark. She had chosen her outfit with care this morning, once David had left the house. She'd laid a dark wool pencil skirt, a cream silk blouse, patent heels and her Sunday best coat on the bed. Once dressed she'd turned to the mirror. Her skirt clung to her hips; her blouse emphasised her breasts. Eva touched her cheek. Applied make-up. Lipstick, mascara, a slash of black eye-liner. She felt good. A rare emotion these days. Vampish, almost. A latter-day heroine. She'd smiled at her silly fantasies and had left the house.

The leather handles of the small overnight bag she carried in her left hand slipped a little as she made her way down the carriage. As the train pulled away from the platform she had to steady herself in the narrow corridor, unused to her heels. Third door down, he'd said. Eva was there now. She hesitated, knocked lightly then pushed the door open slowly. He was there before her, as he'd promised, standing at the window, his back to her.

'Hello,' she whispered.

'You came, then,' he replied, not turning towards her. Without the advantage of seeing his expression she was unsure of his welcome. His voice was deep but toneless. Was he relieved that she was there now? Excited like she was, maybe? She placed her bag by the door, threw her coat onto the narrow bed, then stepped towards him and laid her hand on his shoulder. Only then he turned towards her.

'I'm glad you came,' he said. 'I didn't think you would.'

She was surprised at how sad his lack of faith in her made her feel. They barely knew each other; had only met once before, weeks ago when she was making this same journey. How could he possibly have been certain of her?

He bent to kiss her. Lightly at first, then soon more insistent. She returned his kiss. His lips were soft, warm and dry. She imagined he was responding to her need, doing this for her. After a few moments they stopped and she laid her head on his chest, listening to his heartbeat, feeling the warmth of his body against her cheek. His arms held her close. She breathed deeply, inhaling the light, subtle scent from his cologne. He pushed her away from him. Her heart pounded. This wasn't to be a rejection, surely. She couldn't bear the humiliation. But then he brushed his fingers over her cheek and slipped them under the collar of her blouse. She smiled as he struggled with the tiny buttons with his other hand. They were Mother of pearl, sewn tightly onto the silk. It took an age for him to undo them all and pull her blouse apart. She released her breath; unaware until that moment she had been holding it. Allowing her blouse to slip from her shoulders she willed him to touch her. But he didn't, not right away. Instead his eyes appeared to feast on her, for what felt like an eternity. Then, still silent, he pushed her bra straps from her shoulders and caressed the top of her breasts. She wondered if he could feel the heat radiating from her skin. He reached around her back and released the clasp on her bra, pulling it away from her and discarding it on the bed. He's anticipating my every wish, she thought. He gazed at her exposed breasts. She resisted the temptation to draw her hands across her chest, to cover herself. Then he leant to lick and kiss each nipple. She felt them harden, desire shot through her body. He reached down, pulled her skirt up to her waist. It slid over her thighs. She reached for his belt. He shook his head.

'Not yet,' he whispered.

She had worn her finest silk French knickers, hoping they would please him. He rubbed the palm of his hand over her mound, pulling the fabric into the folds of her cunt, causing her clit to throb with pleasure. His movements were regular and firm. She would come soon if he continued, and it was too soon for her pleasure to be complete, but she was unable to tell him this. Moments before she dissolved he pulled his hand away, hooked a finger into the waistband of her knickers and tore them from her, allowing them to fall silently to the floor, where they lay like a puddle of shimmering rainwater. Looking down at them, Eva could see the wetness of her arousal leaving its mark in their centre. She saw him look down too. And she knew he'd seen the mark. He looked her in the eye, held her gaze. Gave her a small smile. His right hand parted the top of her thighs and he traced his fingers between her legs. His touch was feathery light. She let out a tiny groan.

‘Turn around,’ he said. She gave a nervous glance at the door, it was slightly ajar and the blinds were raised. Would they be seen? She was uncertain whether she cared or not. Everyone on the train was a stranger, after all.

‘Now,’ he said, his voice firm. She guessed he saw surprise cross her face. ‘Please,’ he added, softer this time. Softness in a man was new to her. She felt more tension ease away as his voice caressed her. She turned towards the window. He reached around her and opened it. His body was pressed against hers. But he was still fully clothed. The wool of his suit scratched against her skin. The sensation was surprisingly pleasing. The wind dragged her hair across her face. She shook her head. He pulled her hips back, and she leant her upper body out of the window. The cool air flowed over her breasts and her skin tightened. She shivered in anticipation of his next move, made the more thrilling as she was unable to see him. She reached down to touch herself between her legs, exploring her own heat, bringing the moment of release closer. She felt him reach round to caress her breasts, and she felt spikes of desire course through her body. The knowledge that they were visible to men working in the fields they passed by made her feel surprisingly good. She pushed the fingers of her right hand deep inside herself. She felt the tension that had consumed her earlier in the day had been transformed and was now pulsing through her, soon to be thrust from her body in orgasm. Her wetness ran down her hand. He kissed the back of her neck, pushing her hair aside. One of his hands surrounded her own and pushed it deeper inside her still. She gasped with the pain, the pleasure. His other hand stroked her arse, the top of her thighs. Her legs shook with need and desire.

'I'm ready now,' she said, pleading, hoping he was too.

'Turn around again.' He pulled himself away from her slightly, enabling her to turn towards him, and as she turned she saw him release his trousers and expose his erect cock. He caressed himself momentarily, as if to check his own readiness, and she could see from the glisten of come that he was. She bent to lick it away, savouring the sweet saltiness, and felt him harden against her lips. He gasped. She took him into her mouth, sucking and licking him, feeling his pleasure. After a few moments he pushed her head away gently. He placed his hands around her waist and lifted her, so that she was resting, almost sitting, on the open window ledge. She felt the world rush past her back. The tiny spark of fear of falling onto the track was soon dismissed by the thrill of the newness of her situation. The edge of the frame was digging into her flesh. Her breasts were being bounced by the motion of the train. He caught her right nipple between his teeth. The pain was sharp, echoing that felt across the back of her thighs. She wriggled in an attempt to become comfortable, drew herself forwards. He bent his head down to her, perhaps reading it as an invitation. He parted her legs and began to feast on her wetness. She raised her hands above her head, held onto the top of the window frame to steady herself. If she fell it must not be now, not when complete, enveloping pleasure was threatening to overwhelm her. His tongue lapped up her juices; he pushed it inside her, then rolled over her clit, rhythmically, steadily, slowly building up speed and pressure. She leant back, pressed herself into him, willing him to release her. She threw her head out of the window, aware now, that she would be fully visible to other passengers further back down the train. She felt him lick the full length of her cunt and pull away. Now he's going to fuck me she thought, hoped. He held her hips and pushed his cock inside her, slowly, gently at first. Then, setting his rhythm, he fucked her hard. All her fears were banished now by her desire and her rhythm soon matched his. She pushed herself onto him, pulling him in as deep as she could, filling herself with him, thrusting away any remaining vestiges of anxiety. The waves of her orgasm soon tensed and released through her, demanding she concentrate on pleasure alone. She felt him come too, his thrusts deep and intense inside her. When their pleasure had subsided he pulled her down gently and they clung to each other for a moment. They didn't speak. Then they stood apart from one another.

Eva straightened her skirt and washed her face in the tiny basin. When she turned back to him he had closed the door and lain down on the bed. He reached out his right hand. Relative strangers, they were pressed together now in a strange intimacy on this narrow bed. He stroked her hair back from her face, kissed her forehead and closed his eyes, soon drifting into sleep. Eva remained awake for now. She looked down at the puddle created by her French knickers. A rare present from David they would need to be replaced. She would use some of Aunt Millicent's legacy to buy a new pair. Her inheritance would be released shortly after the funeral she was travelling to,

Aunt Millicent's solicitor had informed her. On the proviso that David never knew of it. Millicent had never approved of him. So Eva had chosen not to tell David of Aunt Millicent's death. Not yet. She knew Millicent would have understood. And that she would have understood Eva's need to make this journey again. At last Eva was ready for sleep, and she rested next to him, dreamless and content.

1001 Arabian Slut Slaves
by Chloe Devlin

LILY STOOD AT THE doorway of the tent, swathed in several layers of a sheer kaftan. As always, she wore what Sultan Ahmed wished. And he'd ordered her to dress and attend to him and his guest.

The Sultan reclined on several large pillows, while his guest sat cross-legged next to him. She was startled to see that his guest was a white man. It was the first white man she'd seen since she'd been abducted. Of course, the only way she knew he was white was because of his blue eyes. Otherwise, he would've been taken for an Arabian, with his sun-baked skin, dressed in the robes of a nomad, with a burnoose around his head.

'Dance for us, Lily Flower,' Ahmed commanded, snapping his fingers.

Lily swallowed and moved further into the warm tent. Trying to hear music inside her head, she began to sway, moving her hips from side to side. She ran her hands up and down her body, stretching the fabric taut against her skin, showing off the shape of her breasts and her hips as she knew Ahmed liked her to do.

He waved his hand for her to continue so she knew

that she was doing things right. Sometimes after just a few seconds he would order her to go away and she would leave in disgrace.

She felt the visitor's eyes follow her every move and she took great care to show off her body's charms, cupping her breasts and brushing her nipples with her thumbs. She knew Ahmed liked it when she played with herself.

At an unspoken nod from her master, she slowly removed the first layer of fabric that was draped over her body. Knowing the two men could catch glimpses of her skin, she continued to sway to some private music inside her head.

The trader shifted from his cross-legged position and stretched out against the cushions, rubbing his crotch. She imagined that he had a long thin cock hidden underneath his robes. Long and thin with a mushroom cap at the top. She figured he had to be circumcised, instead of having a foreskin like Ahmed.

The dancing was starting to arouse her. The thought of servicing this strange man in addition to her master made her hot. Six months ago, she would have been horrified at her thought. But since she'd been kidnapped and held as a pleasure slave in this harem, she'd come to accept her sexual nature.

At Ahmed's signal, she took off the next layer of her kaftan. Now, more of her skin showed through the last two layers of cloth. Her hips began to weave, trying to entice the two men into shedding their clothes too.

The visitor cleared his throat. 'She's beautiful.'

'Wait. It gets better. Lily,' he commanded with a steel thread running through his voice. 'The rest of it, please.'

Lily nodded in acknowledgment. She turned her back to the two men and slowly and sensuously lowered the last two layers of fabric. Inch by inch, her shoulders, then her back was revealed to the two watchers.

Finally, she allowed the fabric to drop entirely, so that she was nude except for her stockings. After letting them get a good look at her smooth buttocks, she turned around. The trader sighed as she grasped her breasts and offered the twin globes to the two men.

She ran her hands all over her body, adding to her growing arousal. Up and down her torso, around her breasts and even over her thighs, letting her fingers stray towards her crotch, but never spreading her legs too wide.

Finally, Ahmed snapped his fingers at her and she stood still, hands at her side. Now was the deciding moment. He would either fuck her or send her back to the harem in disgrace.

Ahmed looked over at his guest. 'Do her looks please you, Joshua? Do you wish to fuck her? Just say the word and we will enjoy her body. If not, I have other slaves in my harem that may be more to your liking.'

The man looked up and down her body once more before replying. 'She'll do. I'd like to fuck her mouth first, if you don't mind.'

Ahmed snapped his fingers again. 'Lily, assume the position.'

As she walked over to the cushions that lay between the two men and stretched out on her back, they stripped off their robes. Unlike Ahmed's thick shaft, the trader's cock was long and thin. Longer even than her Sultan's. A prick that long would reach places inside her that had never been touched. She only hoped that Ahmed would let this stranger fuck her and not arbitrarily change his mind and send her back to the harem.

Ahmed stretched her legs wide apart and began playing with her pussy.

She turned her head towards Joshua and took a deep breath. Before she had finished, the white trader from Assylonia slid his long thin cock deep into her throat. She gulped, taking him even deeper, swabbing her tongue around the head of his shaft.

Ahmed's fingers slid through her pussy lips, spreading her moisture over the slippery skin. The pleasurable touch didn't stop her sucking. Although she knew that Ahmed wasn't touching her for her own enjoyment, her body instinctively responded, her nipples hardening and her sheath spasming.

As she continued to lick and suck on their guest's dick, she remembered the first time she'd been forced to suck Ahmed to climax. It had been several days after her abduction from her carriage. Until that moment, she'd been living in the harem and had seen only the women, no men.

They'd dressed her in a linen robe that was too long, so it dragged on the ground, then led her through the palace to the Sultan. Ahmed had been reclining on a golden lounge chair, his chest bare, an open robe tied loosely around his waist. He'd nodded regally as the head woman had quickly stripped her bare.

She remembered the embarrassment that had flooded her cheeks as she'd tried to hide her private parts with her hands. But at a signal from Ahmed, the head woman had grabbed her hands and held them tightly behind her back, the action thrusting her breasts out. She stood perfectly still, inwardly cringing as he gazed upon her nude body.

Then the head woman had forced her forward until she stood right in front of him. His hands touched her shoulders, pushing her to her knees. He'd opened the robe and drew her head towards his erect member. She'd fought him until he calmly and coolly slapped her across the cheek.

'Suck,' he'd ordered.

Tears filled her eyes. She'd never been hit in her entire life. The slap shocked her so much that she bent her head and did as he ordered, taking his thick shaft into her mouth. The skin of his cock had been surprisingly warm and supple beneath her tongue. With a few grunted commands from him, she'd quickly learned what pleased him.

She'd brought him to climax in her mouth that first time, completely surprised when he ejaculated down her throat. But she'd swallowed it all, unable to jerk her head back. And from there she'd progressed until she was his favourite in the harem. And only favourites got to entertain guests.

A hard thrust brought her back to the present and the two men. Ahmed was shoving two fingers in her pussy, while the trader slammed his cock in and out of her mouth faster and faster.

She felt her orgasm start deep inside her body. As the force of it hit, she arched her body and cried out around the cock in her mouth. The vibrations of her groan brought the man to his climax and he gave one last hard thrust, holding still deep inside her as he spurt his juice several times down her throat.

Ahmed withdrew his fingers, stretching her wide, before leaning back on his cushion. He waited and watched as the trader groaned and reluctantly pulled out of Lily's mouth. She licked her lips, tasting the man's juices lingering there.

'Were you pleased?' Ahmed asked. 'Did she pleasure you?'

Joshua fell back against his own cushions, trying to catch his breath. 'Absolutely. She has one hot mouth.'

Ahmed gave a little smile before rubbing her pussy a few more times. Lily wriggled, trying to get more of his fingers inside her again. 'Yes, she's a tasty little slut slave. If you'd like, you can take her back to your room so you can sample her cunt and ass.'

'Thank you. I'd like that,' Joshua accepted.

A sharp pinch to her clit and labia froze Lily. Even though it was supposed to be a punishment, the tweak of pain felt good and only served to arouse her further, making her hot with desire for this trader.

'That is, if she behaves,' Ahmed said. 'I think you'll find her holes as hot and satisfactory as her mouth.

'And if she misbehaves?'

'If she misbehaves, feel free to punish her, of course.'

Joshua reached over and grabbed Lily's tight nipple between his thumb and forefinger, the pleasurable pain making her wince. 'Oh, don't worry,' he said. 'I think we're going to get along just fine. In fact, with your permission, I think we'll begin now.'

Ahmed released her labia and gave a negligible wave. 'Of course, my friend. Enjoy my Lily Flower.'

Thanking the Sultan, the trader stood, still holding tight to her nipple. 'Come along, slut slave. We have some fucking to do.'

Lily gave her master a lustful look of thanks before following the trader out of the tent for a night of pleasure.

Ecstasy Heights
by Louise Fuller

THE HEAVY POUNDING OF a drum machine matches the beat of my heart as he guides my body through the writhing mass of bodies dancing, arms raised, limbs twitching rhythmically in time to the music.

He grips my wrist tightly as we swerve and slide as smoothly as ice skaters, past people staring blindly at the pulsating lights which throb across the ceiling of the club.

My eyes too are sightless. I am following the heat and scent of his body. My body's movements mirroring his. Finally, like divers breaking the surface of the sea, we burst through the heat and light and noise and enter the cool, still darkness of the night.

We are standing on the edge of the world. On a tiny balcony overlooking a square of apartment buildings.

After the stifling heat of the club, the night air chills the sweat on my skin, causing me to shiver. Below, people on scooters buzz excitedly round the courtyard's narrow roads, and their laughter spirals through the night air. The square is dimly lit by the headlights of the mopeds circling beneath us. Most of the apartments are dark. Their windows gape open blackly to the cooler night air.

Behind the darkness, lying on crumpled beds, the sweat from their bodies already darkening the sheets, I imagine the people who live in the flats. How they move restlessly under the thick blanket of a coming storm.

The air is already damp, and so am I, as he lifts me onto the thick bar of the railings that enclose the balcony.

Holding tightly onto the handrail, I slide backwards and forwards, enjoying the feel of the cool metal on the heat of my thighs.

He presses his body between my knees and pushes up the hem of my skirt. His fingers are firm, their movement assured.

He moves between my legs and gently pushes aside my knickers and spreads the lips of my pussy apart. He draws out a thread of moisture along a curling strand of pubic hair, the back of his hand nudging the hot, swollen flesh between my legs.

Sliding his hands up my back, he traces the bumps of my spine, his fingers splaying and squeezing as I push my hips towards him. I hear myself moan and the sound rolls with the noise of the thunder around the square.

I lean into him, my head spinning as he pulls the shoulder straps of my dress down, exposing my breasts. Pressing his lips to them, he rolls the nipples under his tongue. I moan louder and feel the first drops of moisture on my skin from the storm cloud above.

I close my eyes. Behind me, I can feel the people starting to stir in the darkness of the flats. I imagine them starting to touch themselves, the men rubbing themselves, the women stroking their breasts, their fingers creeping down to their own wetness. I can feel them watching us.

I imagine our bodies reflected hundreds of times in their eyes. He releases his cock from his trousers and rubs the head hard between his fist, sliding up and down the shaft. It stiffens and swells. Reaching out he holds the back of my head to steady me and says, “Put it in”.

I pull his cock into me as the heavy, swollen raindrops start splashing off our bodies.

We thrust towards each other and I groan as he spurts into me. His wetness mixes with my wetness, and then the storm breaks and the warm rain runs over our grateful, panting bodies.

Self-control Lesson
by Anna Ford

HIS VAN HAD ALWAYS been a mystery to Anna. She had only ever been allowed to get things out of it … she had never climbed inside so she had never seen the modifications he had made to it. He had told her to meet him outside his house and already she had been there for ten minutes. She wouldn't dare hurry him along by knocking on the door. Bored, she tries to see inside the van … peering through the driver's window to see if she can see into the back. But dark panelling obscures her view. Still she tries to scan the cab on both sides just to see if she can see anything that reveals more about her Master. From an upstairs window he watches her, smiling at her curiosity and excited about the game he has planned for her over the next few days.

As instructed she has dressed only in her collar, boots and a long leather overcoat. He loves the smell of the leather on her warm body. 'Anna, are you looking for something?'

His powerful voice startles her 'No, Master!' She lowers her head and turns around.

'Don't worry you will soon know the back of this

vehicle well enough.' Unlocking the door he gestures for her to climb in. 'Lift your coat at the back and sit down properly for me.' He smiles at her as she sits down and spreads her knees wide, her hands clasped behind her head and her naked pussy pressing into the seat. 'Good … we aren't going far. I have work to do and you are going to look after my gear while I'm working.'

His words tell her nothing. She doesn't know what his work is, what gear he's talking about or how long this will take. Suddenly he stops the van. She's paid little attention to the journey. She's been concentrating on maintaining her position. They are parked outside a farmhouse and they seem to be alone. 'You may lower your hands and climb down.' He is pleased with the wet patch she has left. He knows very well that she came earlier in the day and the horny little bugger is wet again.

'Take a good look around Anna. Get used to the place you will be here for a few days.'

'Days …? But, Master, I can't be gone for days!'

'You need to do this Anna, you have no control, and you need to learn some. You do not need to worry, I will take care of your affairs.' She can only trust what he says. He opens the back door of the van and nods to her to get in. Her wide eyes look at him in disbelief.

'I'd prefer to stay in the house really if you don't mind!' Hooking his fingers through the rings in her collar he pulls her towards him.

'The van is where you are staying while I work in the buildings … do not worry, Anna, you will have company.'

Obediently she climbs in and instinctively makes

her way to the back of the van. It's dim in there. She can smell wood and oil. Not at all unpleasant to her although she wonders how she will feel after a few days in there. She knows better than to ask him what she will do about food and the other necessary functions of her body. 'On your knees for me, Anna!' Quickly she drops down and stares at the floor. 'Now remove your coat.' She undoes the heavy coat quickly and slides it off her shoulders letting it fall to the floor. She looks perfect, naked at his feet, hands behind her head, the smell of the leather and her pussy making his cock grow hard. No time to fuck her mouth yet, he needs to secure her and get on with his day.

'Good, right on your feet and turn away from me.' He cuffs her hands behind her head and secures the cuffs to the rings in her collar. Then he nods for her to sit on the wooden bench running the length of one side of the van. He then secures the cuffs to a metal ring on the side of the van holding her hands and her head firmly upright. Already she can feel the ache in her arms and she wriggles and twists her body trying not to loose the feeling in her arms and wrists.

'Days, Master, please I can't sit like this for days!'

'Right, Anna you have protested too much. I know you; I know what you are capable of. I have assessed you, trained you and I have brought you this far and you clearly do not trust my judgment of you.' Removing a ball gag from his pocket he pushes it into her mouth and fastens it around her head. 'I expected that I would need to gag you but not so soon, what's wrong with you today?'

She lowers her eyes and sees the spreader bar fixed to the floor. Instinctively she spreads her knees for him and silently he secures her ankles. 'Good girl, Anna, that's much better.'

'Now you will remain in here for three days. I will return every four hours to alter your position and to see to your needs. Every hour during the day I will send one of my friends in to see you. You are not in here to be punished, but to learn. However, I will punish you if you are not willing and compliant. Understand?' Anna nods to him desiring his firm touch on her tits, desiring just the tip of his finger on her clit or a close glimpse of his handsome face before he goes. But he just leaves. As he closes the door on her she sobs through the gag and jerks on her shackled wrists and ankles and twists her hips from side to side. He ignores her and locks the door.

Soon her aching arms go numb. Soon her pussy begins to ache from its stretched position. She tries to focus on her tits; unclamped and unbound they feel good while every other part of her hurts. Once she is focused the hour passes quickly and the first visitor unlocks the van.

'Anna …? I need to check you over.' The man kneels in front of her and inserts his index finger slowly into her aching pussy. She moans at the pleasure as he withdraws and slowly inserts it again. Leaving his finger inside her he raises his head and sucks her nipples more moans escape her gagged mouth. Suddenly he withdraws his finger. 'Very good, Anna but you must practise silence … do not even moan. Control yourself. I will be back in an hour.' Her mind is screaming at him not to leave her in this state. Her pussy is soaked, her nipples hard and she aches for some relief. Again she tries to grind and twist her hips.

There is nothing she can do.

Three times the man returns. Inspecting her pussy always with one finger. Teasing her nipples only with his mouth. By the fourth hour she is expectantly waiting for some relief from her Master. 'I hear that you have remained nicely soaked all morning although not as quiet as I had hoped. I hate keeping you gagged but I think you need it for the rest of the day. Let me look at you.' He pinches each of her lips in his thumb and forefinger and gently pulls open her pussy lowering his head to taste her. She fights not to moan and move her hips. Keeping completely still and silent while he inspects her.

'Good … now I assume you are hungry?' She nods. He unshackles her ankles and unfastens the cuffs from the wall leaving her hands still secured behind her head. He leads her out of the van and towards an outbuilding. Opening the door he tells her to do what she needs. Anna is a little confused at first until she realises she is expected to use the toilet in there. Slowly she understands how lucky she is to at least have this privacy.

Once back in the van he removes the gag and feeds her fruit and water. Then he secures her standing up this time. Ankles again in the spreader bar and hands secured this time to a ring above her head. Every hour a girl comes to inspect her. Inserting her index finger into Anna and sucking and biting at her hardened nipples. Anna maintains her composure and her silence. But each time her pussy is left gaping wide and soaking wet, begging for the relief of an orgasm.

When he returns on the fourth hour her wrists and ankles are freed and he sees to her needs. He nods for her to lie on her back on the blankets he has placed for her on the floor of the van. He tells her to bend her knees, feet flat on the floor. Again he pinches her lips hard stretching her wide and dipping his tongue into her. This time she has no gag and she fights to keep silent and still. 'Well done, Anna. I am pleased with you. I think we can forget the gag now.' He secures her ankles to the spreader bar and cuffs her hands behind her back. Covers her with a blanket and leaves. When he has gone she thrusts her body over so that she is lying face down, takes the blanket into her mouth and screams out her frustration. She sobs and chokes into the material until she finally falls gratefully to sleep.

He stands over her watching her peaceful sleep. Often he finds being this harsh with her difficult. But it improves her, she needs it. He is careful not to break her will, but to let her experience the edge. He kneels behind her and slides his hands under her thighs amused that she has managed to turn over. His thumbs stroke her pussy until she starts to wake up.

'At last he's going to let me cum,' Anna thinks and she lets out a low moan and lifts her ass up towards him. He slaps her hard. 'Did you learn nothing yesterday, you silly girl? Up onto your knees.' She struggles up and he comes to face her. His face is dark and harsh. She keeps her mouth firmly shut not wanting to risk the whole day gagged again. Silently he releases her bonds, his control and power over her making her increasingly wet and desperate for his touch. He guides her to the outbuilding and feeds her. Then he secures her seated on the bench as he did the previous morning. 'Today, Anna, I want you blindfolded.' Her huge eyes plead with him not to do this, not to leave her here at the mercy of strangers, unable to see their faces. It has no effect and he tightens the blindfold around her head.

After the first hour the door opens. 'Hello, Anna, I've been hearing all about you. I understand that you are a wet little slut who cannot keep her mouth shut!' The words turn her cold. She wants to shut her legs. She can almost smell the cruelty of the man. She tries not to gasp as he slaps her pussy with the back of his hand. He twists her nipples and slaps her tits spreading the wetness from her cunt across her chest. Then he digs his fingers into her behind, lifts her up and quickly slides a dildo into her. She is so grateful to be filled at last and not teased by fingers. All too soon he harshly removes the dildo and leaves her. All morning the man visits her using the dildo to work her up and then leaving her. She doesn't make a sound. She stretches and wriggles but she remains silent for him.

The rest of the day passes much the same as the previous day. But by the time her Master returns to settle her to sleep she is hot and wet and almost beside herself. She knows better than to beg him for anything. So she fills her head with the thought that the next day is the third day and surely he will allow her what she needs.

She wakes up early, excited at the prospect of her final day. He unbinds her and sees to her as usual. But to her horror he secures her back in her usual position. 'Today Anna you will remain here all morning alone. No one will visit you.' He leaves her. She is devastated and confused. She begins to wonder if her only way out of this is to escape the next time he unfastens her. She begins to think that maybe he is giving her an opportunity to run each time he takes her to the outbuilding. She convinces herself that it is up to her to make the first move. If she doesn't then no doubt she will face an afternoon alone and a third day without any relief from the burning desire she has to cum. Her pussy is swollen and wet, her nipples red and hard. Her clit feels huge and desperate to be touched. She cannot even close her legs around herself to get any kind of relief.

He returns after four hours, his handsome face smiling down at her. 'You have done better than I thought, but you need more work. I am adding an extra day to our session.' Anna is careful not to let her horror show in her face. He unfastens her and sends her alone into the outbuilding. Anna reasons that she can manage more time and even punishment but she has to get some relief. If she has to stay here anyway how can she make things worse by satisfying herself? Desperate as she is she realises that she doesn't have the time now; already he will be expecting her return. Her only hope is to try and overpower him. To try and use him.

Unusually he is not at the door when she opens it. He must still be in the van. She can hear him on the phone. Someone has distracted him. She could just run now. Her feet will not move. She is frozen. Moisture is running from her .... slipping down her thighs. It's him she wants, what is the point of running? He is sitting with his back to the door, her cuffs just behind him. Without thinking she quickly crawls into the van and quietly lifts the cuffs. He is supporting himself with his left arm behind him as he chats on the phone. She gently fastens one cuff around his wrist and grabs his other arm and fastens his wrists together. 'You devious bitch, Anna. Get these off me NOW!' She has never seen that look before. He frightens her but she has to continue.

Now he is towering above her. She pulls his jeans down to his ankles unbalancing him. She has never even imagined overpowering her Master. His anger is turning her on. She is going to use him. Closing her eyes against the look on his face she pushes him to the floor. He has no hands to stop himself from falling and his ankles are caught up in his jeans. His cock is as hard as she has ever seen it. She is delighted with herself. She has him on the floor before her and she is going to satisfy herself on him.

She stops his protests with her mouth. Kissing him gently until his yells become moans. Then she guides her nipples to his mouth and tells him to suck her gently removing them suddenly when he nips her. 'No, Master I'd prefer you to suck them.' Then she lifts up his T-shirt and she trails her tongue down over his stomach. He is desperate to grab her hair to force her face onto his cock. But she turns her back on him and holds her dripping pussy over his face. 'Suck on my clit, Master.' As she kisses the tip of his cock she lowers her clit towards his mouth. She lets out a low grateful moan as his lips close around her swollen clit and she begins to push back his foreskin with her lips. Usually he would be raking his fingers over her body and pushing his fingers into her pussy. But he can't, he is at her mercy, she is using him. He is desperate to cum inside her pussy not her mouth. But he doubts that he has any control over his own cock even.

Suddenly she stops sucking him and lifts her pussy

off his face. She turns around to face him and stares defiantly straight into his gorgeous eyes as she sinks her pussy down over his thick cock. She pushes down onto him, then places her hands on his chest and lifts her tightening pussy off his cock before pushing back down onto him. He throws his head back moaning that he is going to cum. 'No, Master, you must wait for me!' She pinches her nipples and her clit, fucking him faster. He is holding on so hard for her that she can feel his body shaking.

She feels her pussy begin to spasm as the orgasm she has been held on the edge of for three days begins to surface in her body. 'Now, Master, cum with me NOW!' He opens his mouth and yells her name as he pumps into her tight pussy. She scratches her nails over his chest and throws her head back as she cums over his soaking cock. Exhausted she falls onto his chest. She wants his arms around her but they are not there. So she turns away from him again and resumes her place as his sub. She laps at his wet cock, cleaning him up. Enjoying his twitching body as his cock begins to stiffen again. She wonders if she should leave him there to play with and tease? Probably not … her punishment for this will be harsh enough.

Show Home
by Landon Dixon

WHEN JEN SUGGESTED WE spend another Saturday house-hunting, I was about as excited as a guy preparing for a colonoscopy. But then the headbangers in the upstairs apartment cranked up the Sex Pistols, and I said, "Let's go."

We drove around checking out houses and vacant lots where there could be houses, using a Homebuyers' Guide as our map. And by the time we finally pulled up in front of a show home for what was supposed to be a new semi-rural development, it was already late afternoon. The area currently consisted of the two-storey, red-brick show home, a pair of houses next to it, and a whole lot of bald, empty prairie.

I followed Jen up the flagstone path of the house, not the least bit excited about the development in question, but very excited, as always, by the girl's wrapped-tight, clenching and unclenching butt cheeks. It'd been eight long hours since I'd sexed it up with the blonde, green-eyed beauty in the hot-pink summer dress, and I was hard as the masonry by the time we walked through the front door of the house.

An estate agent was lying in wait, and she gave us

her spiel as she showed us around the vacant home. Then, when she had to answer the call of her cell, she left Jen and me alone to explore an upstairs bedroom.

"Oh, look!" Jen yelped, pointing out the window.

I was looking, all right – at my girl's firm, handful tits and taut, round bottom, her wicked body showing spectacularly in that thigh-slit shorty dress. I walked over to her, wrapped my loving arms around her waist and squeezed her tight. Then I followed her finger downwards, into the backyard of the house next door, and got a whole new appreciation for the term 'Neighbourhood Watch'.

An attractive young couple was getting busy with each other right out there in the sun-drenched open! The guy was on his knees in the newly laid sod, hands gripping the redheaded babe's ass, face buried in between her long, slender, visibly shaking legs. She was up against the wall of their dream home, one hand riding the guy's blond head, the other feeling up her big, bronze tits, rolling her jutting, mocha nipples. Bathing suits lay abandoned on the lawn; I guess the lusty pair had intended to go for a dip in their swimming pool to cool off, and never made it.

They must've thought they were hidden from public consumption by the eight-foot-high cedar fence that surrounded their backyard, and I guess they were – from ground-level, at least. But not from where Jen and I were standing and watching, getting way excited.

I pressed my steel-hard cock into Jen's plush derriere as I ogled the sexy scene below, saw the busty redhead's mouth open and eyes close and body jerk as her lover turned up the tongue-torque on her pussy. I squeezed Jen even tighter, breathing in the girl's sweet,

sweet body spray, feeling her heat. Sexual electricity surged through me, lighting a bulb over my head.

"Let's do what they're doing," I proposed, brushing Jen's hair back and kissing her neck, nibbling her cute, little ear. "It's the neighbourly thing to do."

She giggled. I dropped to my knees and shoved up the hem of her dress, grabbed onto her big, bold butt cheeks and licked the cotton crotch of her pink panties, turning them and her wet at the same time. She moaned and spread her legs wider apart, clutched at my hair.

"He's really licking her," she breathed, staring out the window. She fumbled the straps of her dress off her shoulders, cupped one of her boobs and squeezed.

I tore the girl's panties apart and speared her exposed sex with my tongue. Her butt cheeks jumped in my hands, and I dug my tongue deeper into her dripping puss, wriggled it around inside her.

"Yes!" she groaned, legs quivering, working her tits.

I lapped hungrily at her pussy, hard-licking her from her arsehole to clit over and over.

"Now he's finger-fucking her!" Jen squealed.

I ploughed two digits into my girl's pussy and sawed away, tonguing her clit as I pumped her.

"She's coming! She's coming!" Jen wailed, her sun-kissed, sweat-dappled body shaking out-of-control as I relentlessly tongued and furiously finger-fucked her to matching orgasm. She came in my mouth, drenching me with her juices.

Then it was my turn to provide the play-by-play, Jen to act it out. The busty redhead was on her knees in the grass now, her man's thick cock in her mouth. She slid her cherry lips back and forth on his shaft, expertly blowing him.

I popped my jeans open and Jen yanked them down. She tugged my stiff-as-a-board prick out of my shorts and stroked it with her hot little hands. Then she popped my mushroomed hood into her warm, wet mouth and started sucking.

"Fuck!" I groaned, watching the carnal couple next door, watching Jen earnestly bob her blonde head up and down on my pulsing prick. "She's deep-throating him!" I hollered.

Jen swallowed my lie, swallowed me, inching her lips down my shaft till her nose was all but buried in my pubes. My legs turned to jelly and my knees buckled, my throbbing cock locked in Jen's wet, tight mouth and throat. I grabbed her hair for support.

Then the babe next door suddenly pulled her guy's greasy rod out of her mouth and cranked it with her hand, jacking him. Her hand became a blur on his slickened pole, and he yelled out and jerked around and sprayed hot cum all over her pretty face and tits.

I ploughed my raging cock back and forth in my girl's mouth, going faster and faster. Then my balls tightened and my muscles locked and I blasted sizzling semen straight down Jen's throat, emptying my balls with such force and length that I almost passed out.

Someone coughed. I twisted my head around and saw our long-forgotten estate agent standing in the doorway, studying her shoes. Jen and I bought the property directly north of the redhead's house. Then, when we were driving away, we were surprised to see the agent shaking hands with our soon-to-be new, now fully clothed, neighbours.

Spying on Audrey
by Eva Hore

I WROTE A WHILE back telling you about my neighbour, Audrey, the school teacher, who used my pool when I wasn't there. Well, I thought I'd fill you in on what's been happening since. You'll remember that I took advantage of her, fucking her from behind when she thought I was her boyfriend.

Well, not long after this, I found myself constantly thinking about her. I knew she was home alone as I'd been watching her house all day, all week for that matter. It was the school holidays and she hadn't left the house since I'd fucked her.

That night I saw her bathroom light go on. I ran up my stairs to peek down from the upstairs window. I only caught glimpses of her though, the steam from the shower fogging up the overhead window. My persistence paid off though when I saw her enter her bedroom, clad only in her towel. She didn't even bother closing the drapes which was strange as she was usually so strict about that sort of thing.

Running back downstairs I sidled up to my dining room window which was adjacent to her bedroom. She was lying on the bed, still naked, flipping through some magazines. I wondered if they were porn magazines, if she was getting herself in the mood for some masturbating.

I hoped so.

The fact that she'd left the drapes open meant to me that she was inviting me in so I thought I'd take the chance and see if the back door was open.

It was.

Opening the door and closing it firmly behind me I crept down the passage. Her bedroom door was also ajar. I could hear the rustling of the pages as she flipped them over. As quietly as I could, I inched my way forward until I was at the edge of the doorway. A low buzzing noise confirmed my suspicions. She was using a vibrator to get herself off.

I licked my lips nervously as I peeked around the door. She was lying in the centre of the bed, her dark hair spilling over the pillow. She was pushing the vibrator in and out of her pussy, her hairless pussy. I nearly gasped when I saw it. I wondered if she'd done it for me, if this whole business about leaving the drapes open was to lure me over here.

I most certainly hoped so.

I peeked back in. She was running the vibrator over her clit, moaning softly. She needed more than a vibrator. She needed me in there to give her a good fucking. I shucked out of my clothes, standing there naked as my cock throbbed and pulsated, eager to sink into her hot cunt.

'Come on,' she moaned and I wondered if she was speaking to me, if she knew I was there.

A peek through the crack in the door and I saw her pulling the hood back from over her clit. She was rubbing furiously, obviously unable to orgasm. Her head fell back, her eyes closed and her rubbing became more focused. I knew it was time to make my presence known.

Without any hesitation I threw myself between her open thighs and sunk my cock straight in. Her eyes opened wide, for a second only, and then her legs were wrapping themselves around my back, her heels digging into me as she encouraged me along.

'Harder,' she demanded. 'Fuck me harder.'

I slammed into her. Her tits and flesh jiggled all over the place. I lowered my head trying to latch onto a nipple but wasn't able to. She lifted a breast up towards my eager mouth and I sucked deeply, biting down on the nipple as saliva pooled in my mouth.

'Oh, yes,' she moaned. 'Yes, yes.'

Fuck, she was like a madwoman, kicking into me while her fingers clawed at my chest, raking the nails down to tug at my pubic hair before grabbing painfully at my balls.

'Flip over,' I demanded.

She didn't hesitate. I grabbed hold of her hips and my cock found its way back in easily. Now that she was up on all fours it was easier for me to grab her breasts. I crushed them cruelly, enjoying her screams of pleasure as her arse ground back into me.

I thrust further forward, slapping at her hips, her thighs. Her juices gushed around my electrified cock as she screamed her release. She went crazy then, grabbing me and throwing me on my back. She straddled me, impaling herself upon my mighty cock.

Grinding her pussy down hard into my pelvis she bent forward, squashing her breasts against my hairy chest. I ran my hands over her back, her arse, then further over her crack to tantalised her puckered hole. She wiggled against my fingers and I inched on in, then another until I was finger-fucking her arse.

She came in gallons all over me, her juices pooling down to run over my balls before saturating the bed. Pinching my nipples firmly between her fingers she demanded I come. I was happy to oblige and shot my load high into her pussy.

We lay there together gasping for breath. She had the stamina of a hundred women and in no time was pulling me off the bed and into her shower, our hands slipping crazily over our lathered skin. Her fingers were cupping my balls, then stroking my cock before she kneeled on the floor, the water washing over her hair and face as she sucked me off.

Never in my life have I ever been so deliciously fucked. Now whenever I see her drapes open I know it's time to come over. And, to tell you the truth, in the last month they've only been closed once and that was when she had her mother staying over.

I must say though, her mother's extremely good-looking for her age and the thought of a threesome is most appealing.

Who knows, perhaps I'll be writing to you again.

Watch on the Danube
by Donna George Storey

'YOU'LL NEVER BELIEVE WHAT that man just did to that woman over there.' Pru meant to whisper, but the excitement in her voice seemed to echo through the grand hotel dining room.

Adam glanced over his shoulder toward the couple at the table by the window, the one with the best view of the river.

'Don't stare at them,' Pru hissed, blushing.

'*You're* staring at them,' Adam said, taking another bite of his roll.

Pru was about to argue that she was only gazing wistfully at the Danube and the couple happened to be in the way, but she didn't want to cause any more of a scene. She dropped her eyes to her own plate, still a foreign vision in itself with the crusty roll and slices of ham and cheese. It was a typical Central European breakfast, although it would be lunch back home and gave her a stomach ache so early in the morning. Still, Pru believed an enlightened traveller did her best to adapt to local custom.

'So, what did he do?' Adam asked, still chewing.

'He kissed her hand,' Pru said in a low voice,

feigning interest in her breakfast.

Adam arched an eyebrow, his 'yeah, so?' expression.

'Well, it wasn't a joke. When that woman walked in to the dining room he stood and took her hand and bowed and kissed it, or let his lips hover an inch away and pretended to kiss it, or whatever they do when they know what they're doing. Which he obviously does.'

'It's a castle hotel. Rich, pretentious people stay here. Lucky for us we got an off-season discount.'

'They're not just rich,' Pru insisted. 'This is breeding. She's probably a baroness. Maybe the last of the Hapsburg line.'

Adam rolled his eyes. He had a small blob of jam at the corner of his mouth. Pru dabbed at her own mouth with her napkin to alert him, but he was too busy pouring more coffee to notice.

She resumed her engrossed-in-the-view-of-the-Danube pose so she could study the couple further. They were an unusual pair. The woman was at least forty, painfully slender and pale. By contrast, her jet-black hair was glossy and full, cut elegantly to graze the jaw line. Her wide-set eyes suggested Jackie O. She was not pretty, but there was something about her – centuries of refinement steeped in her bones – that made Pru long to climb into her fine wool suit for a moment to *be* her.

The man was obviously several years younger and powerfully built beneath his Armani jacket. He was also very good-looking – blond, sportsman's tan, chiselled features – and Pru would have described him as L.A. if it weren't for his flair for kissing ladies' hands which put him in a very different class altogether.

The couple leaned toward each other, caught up in their conversation. They spoke in German, but Pru couldn't catch any of the words she'd memorised from the Berlitz guide. She noticed, too, that after that hand kiss, they never touched.

Suddenly, the man glanced up – perhaps she *had* been staring? – and for an instant their gazes locked. That's exactly how Pru felt, bound fast by his chilly blue eyes. She was accustomed to admiring looks from men, but this was different. His eyes merely passed over her as they might a butter knife or a pot of coffee, an object to be coolly dismissed.

To her dismay, Pru realised she felt warm and tingly between her legs. But before the warmth reached her cheeks in a blush, the man had looked away.

Later that morning, Pru and Adam hiked up to the ruins of the medieval fortress where Richard the Lionheart had been held captive on his way back from the Crusades. Pru wanted to linger and contemplate the same view Richard himself had gazed upon 800 years before – the dark blue river snaking through the vineyards and villages of the Wachau – but Adam argued that the best way to honour the king's memory was to escape back to town for a hearty lunch.

As Pru followed him grudgingly down the path, she mused that while they got along quite well back home, their first overseas trip was presenting new challenges. Adam's software engineer's skills were useful when it came to navigating strange cities and rattling off facts from the guidebook, but he always seemed on edge, even defensive, in spite of his constant jokes about the local customs. He couldn't see the magic that enchanted her: the history pulsing within castle stones, the ghosts lurking in the moss greens and greys of the late autumn landscape, the breathtaking thrill of watching a man actually kiss a woman's hand.

Sometimes she wondered if they'd gone on completely different trips altogether.

Adam did redeem himself somewhat at the restaurant when he pointed out the baroness and her lover tucked away in a shadowy corner. Fortunately, this time he only jerked his chin discreetly in their direction. 'Your friends are here. You take that seat so you can keep a look out for any more strange, antiquated behaviours.'

Pru wrinkled her nose at him, but she did take the chair that gave the better view. 'She's daintily picking at some kind of fish. I think he has the duck with dumplings and red cabbage.'

'That's what I'll have then. What's good enough for the baron is good enough for me.'

'Oh, he's not a baron. He has a touch of nobility, but she's the one with the blue blood.'

'You might be right. Her skin's so pale, she does look a bit blue, like skimmed milk. It's creepy.'

Pru glanced over at the baroness, who was bringing another morsel of fish to her lips with the utmost delicacy. There was no pretext to be staring at them here, but they seemed too wrapped up in each other to notice. And yet Pru's heart was beating faster, as if she *wanted* them to catch her.

Suddenly the ring tone of a cell phone trilled through the empty restaurant. Pru jumped. The baroness did, too. She took her phone from her leather handbag and seemed to stiffen when she read the caller ID. Immediately she rose from her chair and rushed outside.

'Her husband's just called,' Pru whispered.

'Husband?'

'Oh, yes. He's much older and he's been impotent for years and she's having a wild affair with this young stud to keep herself from going crazy from a lack of sex. But if she gets caught, it will cause a terrible scandal.'

'You have some imagination,' Adam snorted, but he looked amused, too.

The waiter appeared with his duck and her fish. While Adam tucked in to the dumplings, Pru couldn't help looking over at the table in the corner once more.

This time the man was staring right at her, and again she had that odd feeling of being frozen in place by his dismissive gaze. In the next moment, his expression softened and his lips twitched into a smile. He did find her attractive, she thought with some relief, but even that familiar glimmer of male desire was tempered with hauteur.

'I'm just a peasant to him, but he'd use me for his pleasure if nothing better were at hand.' Pru felt a clutch of anger in her belly at the thought of his lordly arrogance, but then she realised she was feeling other things, too. The fabric of her bra chafed at her stiffened nipples and her panties were undeniably damp, as if her own body longed to be used in just that way. She could almost see it happen, the smirk of entitlement on his lips as he rammed her squirming body with his sceptre, leaving nothing but a gob of spunk in her pussy and a smack on her bare ass as parting thanks.

It was as if he really did hold the power to touch her and move her with his eyes alone.

The baroness and her lover failed to make an appearance in the hotel dining room that evening. Unable to hide her disappointment, Pru picked at her roast pheasant, barely managing to smile agreement when Adam suggested they skip dessert to go make love.

When they got back to their room, Adam went off to brush his teeth, while Pru walked over to the sliding glass doors and pressed her fingers to the cool glass. Her eyes drank in the twinkling lights of the town on the far bank blending into the stars and the great Danube River rushing through the night, as if drawn ever onward by some dark, searching hunger.

That's when she saw them, silhouetted against a golden square of window floating high in the tower suite across the courtyard. She could only make out their shadowy forms, but she knew it was the baroness and her lover, her slight figure in front, his muscular body behind. At first it just looked like the couple was taking in the enchanting night view, but as her eyes adjusted, Pru noticed that they were swaying rhythmically, moving together toward the window then back again.

'Oh my God, Adam, I think they're actually fucking out there.'

'Who? The anorexic vampire and her bodyguard?' Adam called from the bathroom. 'Are they doing it on our balcony?'

'It's almost as bad. They're screwing in front of their window with the lights on.'

In an instant he was beside her, dressed in the hotel's thick terry robe, smelling of toothpaste. He squinted up at the window. 'Too bad we didn't bring the binoculars.'

The couple had, apparently, finally done something to earn his attention.

Pru felt her cheeks go hot. 'Turn off the light. They'll see us watching.'

Adam just grinned. 'That's probably why they're doing it.'

Pru snapped off the bedside lamp. The room fell into darkness, lit only by the glow of the bathroom light. 'Don't you understand? Peasants like us don't count. If they're showing off, it's for the ghosts of her Hapsburg ancestors. Or the great Danube. Or history itself.'

Adam didn't snicker, as she feared he might. He gazed up at the couple, still moving together in their slow, subtle dance.

'I think they do need us, Pru. It's more exciting for them if the lower orders are around to watch their performance.' He stepped behind her. She could feel his erection through the robe. Still slightly woozy from the wine at dinner, an image flashed into her head – she and Adam stepping onto a boat together and gliding off through a thick, warm mist.

Before she was quite aware of what he was doing, Adam had unbuttoned her shirt. His fingers groped for the clasp of her bra.

'What are you doing?' She tried to turn around, but his arms held her in place.

'Well, as you always say, we should do what the locals do, and the locals here seem to have a custom of fucking at their hotel windows.'

'But someone might see,' she protested, squirming.

'Only your friends up there, and you want them to see,' he crooned, taking advantage of her movements to pull the shirt over her arms and slide the bra off. 'There, don't you want to show them your beautiful tits? They're bigger than hers and so sensitive. All I have to do is play with them and I know you'll be begging me to stick it in.' He began rolling her stiff nipples between his fingers.

Pru moaned. Her flesh burned with shame and arousal. But Adam was right. She did want them to see her. She wanted to touch them as they had touched her.

'Now put your hands back on the glass, Pru, and lean forward so your ass sticks out just like her ladyship,' Adam said.

Slowly, as if in a dream, Pru pressed her palms to the window and pushed her buttocks out in offering. Adam yanked down her pants and slipped his finger between her lips. He began to tease her clit with languid strokes.

She gasped with pleasure, but a tiny voice of caution still lingering in her brain bleated out, 'What if we do get caught?'

Adam laughed. 'As far as I can tell, there's no one else staying here tonight but her ladyship and her stud, and they won't be telling on us. Besides, don't we servants get to have a little fun now and then? I get so tired spending all my time fussing with his cufflinks, and straightening his ascot, and seeing his hairy ass when he steps into the bathtub. And I notice the way she treats you, never happy with anything you do, as if she could last a day without your services. How could we survive if we didn't snatch a bit of fun in the linen closet now and then?'

Pru's knees wobbled, as if Adam had suddenly steered the boat into uncharted waters. Servants? Ah, yes, he was making up a fantasy. Who ever dreamed Adam had it in him? Her mind leaped to the game like a clit rises to a knowing touch. In an instant, Adam's fingers were no longer rubbing bare pussy, they were snaking over garters and through the opening of her drawers. His other hand was tweaking a nipple that poked out over a corset. And his robe had dissolved into the uniform of a valet who was making hurried love to the lady's maid in a closet, both of them knowing they didn't have much time before they were called them back to duty.

'We have to finish quickly,' she murmured, taking up her cue. 'My lady will punish me terribly if she sees.'

Adam immediately picked up the pace, working her clit so the room was filled with the steady click of finger on wet flesh. 'Don't you know they've been watching you all along, Pru? I've seen the master staring at your luscious bosom and your high, round ass. And she wants you even more. Do you notice how she flushes when you help her dress, how she finds any excuse to order you to powder her neck or fix her garters? Now that you've shown yourself to be more shameless than they'd ever imagined, they can't take their eyes away.'

'But wouldn't they want ...' Pru faltered. Would Adam let her take the rudder and guide the boat on a new course? She gulped and pushed the words out. 'Wouldn't they ... want to punish us?'

'Oh, yes, they'd want to punish a trollop like you.'

'And you, too, for seducing me. So, they'd take me to bed with them and … make you watch.'

Adam seemed to hold his breath. Then he exhaled in a soft moan.

Pru's voice grew bolder. 'They make you stand in the corner with your cock straining in your trousers as they undress me and lay me out on the bed. Then she takes out her powder puff, the one I use to touch up her complexion before she goes to dinner, and she rubs it over my breasts.'

Adam moaned again, louder this time.

'I'm so turned on from what you've done to me in the closet, and what she's doing – the soft friction on my nipples is driving me crazy – that I start begging them to touch me between my legs. She refuses. She says she wants me to kiss her breasts first. She holds her one of her little lavender nipples out to me, and I take it in my mouth and suckle, and she arches back in her pleasure and stares right at you, taunting you, because she has more power over me than you do.'

'Fuck,' Adam breathed. He took his cock in his hand and began probing Pru's cunt with the swollen head.

'The master is saying he wants to fuck me to give me my proper punishment, but she has him under her heel, too, and she tells him, no, but he can take her from behind and watch while she eats me to climax.'

Adam pushed inside her with a soft suck of wetness.

'And you've pulled your dick out and you're rubbing yourself and they're too caught up in their own wickedness to order you to stop.'

Adam was thrusting steadily now, his fingers still

working her clit and nipple with frantic urgency.

'But you have the best view of all because you can see me lying with my legs spread wide, my glistening red slit exposed, and you can see the pink crack between her buttocks spread as she bends over and starts to lap at me like a little cat, and you can see him push his tool inside her. It's shorter than yours but thick, and she gasps as he enters her. She looks up, her mouth dripping because I'm so wet, and she commands me to play with my breasts while she licks me. And the master, he's so mesmerised by his wife's brazenness that his cock seems to wilt as he stands there. Good servant that you are, you know exactly what he needs, so you take one of his leather gloves that he's tossed on the floor with his clothes and you start spanking him with it just like the head master at his old boarding school. Suddenly he's rock hard again and he starts slamming into her with each smack of the glove, and then he comes, and she comes and I come …'

Apparently Adam was, too. He groaned, one hand slapping her buttock in a flurry of blows as he emptied himself into her.

Pru wiggled her hips triumphantly and gazed up at the window. The couple was still there, standing side by side now, their figures dark against the golden backlight. Then the woman raised her hand – a salute, perhaps, or was she only fixing her hair? – and they disappeared from view.

Adam pulled the curtain closed. They sank back on the bed together.

'Damn you and your wild stories,' he whispered with a grin. 'I was planning to make you come first and save myself for the second act. But I'm beginning to see the advantage of going with the flow when you travel to a foreign land.'

Pru smiled. Tomorrow's destination was decadent Vienna, then the charming streets of Budapest. And then, wherever the river took them, now that Adam could see it, too – all the surprising and marvellous things a man could do for a woman and she could do for him.

She was looking forward to the journey.

Scrapbook Pages
by Sommer Marsden

I WATCH THEM RUNNING in the water. Hear their laughter. I check my watch. Ten thirty.

Simon douses Paige with a bucket of water. She shrieks and runs to me, laughing all the way.

'Mom! He just dumped water on me.' It is meant to be a tattle but she is grinning too much to pull it off.

'I saw.'

'Well?' She cocks her hip and settles her little fist there. 'Isn't he in trouble?' At eight she thinks she is his second mother.

'You'd have to stop smiling in order for him to be in trouble. A tear or two might do the trick.' I wink.

'Fine!' she huffs but then she giggles and runs back to the surf.

Simon stands, shielding his eyes from the sun. Gauging whether or not he is in trouble. I wave and smile and his shoulders relax. I put my forehead down and feel the sun on my back. I check my watch again. Five minutes have passed. A familiar twist of excitement wiggles low in my belly. Soon.

I hear Simon yell and then Paige's victorious, 'Take that!' I laugh into the beach towel. For all their fake bickering they are having a blast.

I do not check my watch again. I will not. Cannot. I wait and let the large expanse of skin I have chosen to show this year brown in the sun. I adjust my brown and blue bikini, one I am very proud to be looking pretty decent in this year. I am fidgeting and I know it, but I will not check the time.

I hear approaching feet. That shifting sand sound of someone walking on too hot sand.

'We are here, my dear!' my mother chirps. I look up and blink at the bright light.

'Hey, Ma. Hey, Dad.'

My parents settle their beach chairs, their cooler, their umbrella and their bags. They look ready for a safari as opposed to an hour or two babysitting on the beach.

'How are they today?' my father asks, jabbing the beach umbrella deep into the sand so it will stand straight.

'Having a blast. Thanks for doing this every day.' When I say it I feel a sudden bite of guilt in my chest. If only they knew.

'Not a problem. It's your vacation, too,' my mother chatters merrily. She unpacks the cooler, having packed a feast for her grandchildren. 'You deserve a little alone time. If only Alan could have come. He could use a vacation, as well.'

'Well, he never comes,' I say, careful to keep my voice even. 'By choice. He chooses not to be a part of the family vacations.'

My mother nods, her lips pressed into a tight seam. She knows I'm right but she won't comment. You just don't do that. Say something bad about the man of the house. My father acts as if he hasn't heard.

'You sure you won't stay and have some chicken and potato salad before your walk?' she asks. As she says it, I see motion from the corner of my eye. There he is. He sets up his chair, puts his book on the seat and looks out to the water. For all intents and purposes, I am invisible.

'No thanks,' I manage, my gaze clinging to the broad brown expanse of his shoulders. The place at the small of his back where the sweat pools and glistens. 'I'm ready for my walk. Not hungry.'

I give all four of them a kiss before I go. I walk along the sand near the water where it's packed and hard. My feet dig little divots in the dark grey shore. I don't turn around and look but I can feel him behind me. That fake shiver that seems so out of place in blazing heat overtakes me. That moment where your body gets confused and breaks out in goosebumps while sweating profusely. This time it isn't just intense heat. He's set it off. Him and what we are about to do. Again.

I walk further down the beach. Further than the day before. Every day I go a little longer before stopping. My eyes roam wildly, judging and dismissing locations. Finally, I see something. An abandoned wooden structure. It had probably been a lifeguard shack at one point. Now there are no lifeguards on the beach. They make sure you know by posting a sign to that effect every hundred feet or so.

This part of the beach is nearly deserted but I still make an effort to be nonchalant as I veer from the shoreline toward the shack. The wood is rough and grey from the salt air. The door is hanging off at an angle. Who knows what might inhabit the inside.

As I walk up each step, I wonder if I'll get a splinter. I stop wondering when I hear his heavy footsteps behind me. My skin rises up in little hard peaks again and my nipples constrict. The dampness of my bikini bottom is no match for the dampness seeping from my body now. I shake off the chill and I turn to face him.

Fierce green eyes, dark brown hair. Tan and lean and smiling a predator's smile. His name is Will. Just Will. I have not asked his last name and I have no intention of doing so.

I open my mouth to say something and he covers it with his own before I can speak. I give into the kiss, letting him thrust his tongue around and force mine into submission. Will does everything roughly. I like it that way. No tender interludes to fuck up the memories or egg on the guilt.

His fingers dig into my top and pinch my nipples. The pleasure and pain dance along my nerve endings, pooling in my groin. A fiery pulse starts in my cunt because in my mind I can see his cock. I remember yesterday. The frantic coupling in a field of sea oats and the pulse ratchets up to a thumping that is maddening.

I grab at his low slung short, push at the waistband. When I find the hard smooth flesh of his cock I stroke it. He is hot in my hands. Not hot from the sun but from blood flow and want. He breaks the kiss and bites along my throat, not hard enough to leave any marks but hard enough that he knows I will grow wet enough for him to be harsh with me.

My back scrapes against the rough wood and it

flashes through my mind that someone might walk up on us. See us. Know we are here. And then that thought fades because his blunt fingers worm down into my bottoms to find the humid heat they seek. He slides two fingers into my pussy and I moan against his shoulder. He adds a third and I bite him. Hard. He doesn't care. No one will question him later. He is single. That much I know.

'Help me, Jill,' he growls in my ear because the damn nylon is sticking to my skin and creating a resistance. I help him but my mouth hasn't stopped on his shoulder. He tastes like coconut lotion and sun and salt on my tongue.

Then there we are. My bottoms slung right below my ass cheeks. That part of me stark white against the brown skin kissed by the sun. His shorts are down around his knees. He kicks them to the side and on his way to standing straight, yanks my bottoms all the way down. I step out of them.

One hand finds my thigh, pulls it up, wraps it around his waist. He holds me like that. An unfaithful stork, balanced on one foot, being fucked in public. That shoots another ball of heat through my centre and he forces into me. Thrusting up high and hard. His eyes boring into mine. He likes to watch me as he fucks me. He likes to watch me come. He even likes the one or two tears that may escape when all is said and done.

'Tomorrow's your last day here,' he says bluntly. His teeth find my nipple and tear at it.

I feel that familiar tightening in my cunt. The pulse becomes a flutter. The pounding gets faster and rougher. He bites again and I moan and clutch at him.

'Yes. My last day.'

'We're walking tomorrow?' he asks, staring me down again. Biting his fingers into my waist, pushing me roughly against the wood.

His cock is hitting me just right inside and when he yanks my leg higher I start to unfold. Little pieces of light taking up more and more of the space inside of me that is normally dark.

'Yes!' I say as I come. It is both an answer to his question and a declaration of joy for those moments where I feel alive. When I come. When a man wants me. Really wants me. Where I am not a piece of scenery or a secretary.

Two, three, four more heavy thrusts and he empties into me with what is possibly the harshest sound I have ever heard from a human throat.

We both dress. He's still staring and I like it. I like that he keeps his eyes on me until he isn't allowed to anymore. I don't kiss him. I never do once it's over. He walks off first. That is what I stipulated a week ago on day one.

I stare at the shack. Its weathered beauty. Its stark design. I will come back later and take a picture. The walk back is pleasant. My body warm inside and out. My skin feels like warm liquid. I can feel his come puddling in the cotton crotch of my bikini bottom.

Back at the blanket, I accept the lunch my mother offers. I listen to the kids chatter and I laugh. I also stare at the back of Will's head as he sits and read his book not twenty feet away. He will still be sitting there when we leave. His close proximity and the knowledge of our recent act keeps my nipples hard throughout the afternoon. No one but me knows, the top is well-padded. He might suspect it but he will never tell.

I'm putting the finishing touches on the last scrapbook page when Alan walks in. He gives me a chaste kiss on the back of the neck.

'I'm really sorry I couldn't make this one,' he says, looking over my shoulder. 'I can't wait to look at the completed book.'

He says *this one* as if he has ever made a family vacation. In nine years, he never has. I've been nearly invisible for two years. I am not a financial spreadsheet or the head of a major corporation. I am unimportant.

'I know. Maybe next year,' I say with a small smile. I can do the dance of insincerity as well. I have mastered it.

I slide the twelve by twelve paper into the protective sleeve and shut the book. When he holds out his hands and grins as if he truly cannot wait to see it, I hand it over.

We will look at it together like we always do.

He flips through and laughs at the picture of Simon and Paige mugging for the camera with the fish they just caught. He smiles at the picture of my parents in a dance contest at a restaurant. Then he points to the lone picture on one page. A rickety white flight of wooden steps.

'These are my favourites,' he says, pointing. 'The ones where you just take pictures of things. You have a way with the camera. They have so much feeling in them.'

I nod and look over his shoulder. They are my favourites too. When he looks at the picture he sees weathered steps looking very artistic. When I look at the picture, I see myself on my knees under that staircase, Will's cock in my mouth. I see my face covered in his come. I see it hanging off my earlobes like pearl earrings. And I see him pulling my bathing suit down and eating my pussy. I smile again.

'And this one,' he points and beams at me. Wifey *can* do something after all. She can take pictures.

I glance and smile back. The field of sea oats. I look at the picture and see Will fucking me from behind. Leaving vivid white fingerprints on the mocha-coloured skin of my hips. I see him grabbing my hair and yanking my head back as he pounds his cock into me and I hear him saying, 'Fuck. You feel so good, Jill.'

That is what *I* see. What *I* hear.

There are eight of these pictures. Each one is magical to me. I do not see what he sees when he looks at them. I see what happened there. I remember that feeling of being wanted.

Alan turns to the lifeguard shack.

'Ah,' I say with a little laugh. 'That is *my* favourite.'

He nods and agrees and continues on looking at my stay-at-home mum handiwork. This is my fifth album. There will be more unless he makes the next one.

I close my eyes and feel a big hand hook my naked leg around a warm waist. I hear slapping fucking sounds. I smell coconut. I hear sounds only animals should make. I feel warm semen leaking from me. And my skin feels like warm liquid again for just a moment.

A Punishment to Some
by Anaïs Nohant

A REGULAR TÊTE-À-TÊTE SEEMED out of the question now. Defying *his* rules meant discipline would become the game of today's lesson. This was my first confrontation with the primal side of the man I called DH. The secret side buried under his wit and facade of emotional vacancy.

I had actually dared not to wear his favourite toy in his presence. I did not, in point of fact, want to disregard his request to prepare myself for him. Quite the opposite. I thought that with me wearing a flowing white cotton skirt, surely someone would know – would see. The coward in me felt like I couldn't risk it. Never in my wildest dreams would I have thought he would suspect or even intuitively know. Even harder for me to imagine that he, as we stood together in front of our suburban coffee shop, would check when I least suspected it.

Aided by the sound of whizzing cars, and caffeine-addicted patrons' eyes glued to their electronic gadgetry, oblivious, he proceeded with great stealth to slip a warm and soft hand under my bare cunt towards my backside. I had failed to do his bidding and he now knew it.

Eyes squinting and mouth hardened, his stoic facial expression developed a deliberate cold look of infuriation. He grabbed my hand, my purse, my keys and almost dragged me to my car. I tried to explain. He lifted his hand to say *not now*. I had no idea where he was going until we hit the red light. Then I thought that maybe he was taking me to the park near my house. When he passed that street, and turned onto mine, my breath hitched. I couldn't believe it. He knew where I lived.

Without saying a word, he parked the car and killed the engine. Within two seconds, he was at the passenger side, beckoning me to exit. He grabbed my hand again, pulling me to my front door. As he unlocked and opened the door, I peered nervously over his shoulder to check if anyone noticed our entrance. He nudged me to the dining room. Light blasted from all the windows. 'Off, take it all off now!' he said, assuming a predatory stance. My eyes flew to the windows. Was he not the least alarmed by our visibility to all?

'Don't defy my wishes again,' he ordered.

I opened my mouth to speak, but he never gave me the chance. Clothes flew everywhere before my mind had the ability to assimilate what was happening. He pressed me down on the middle of my glass dining table. The abrasive sound of him jerking his tie from its confines made a shiver run down the length of my spine. Without penitence, he secured my hands behind my back. He took his hand and rubbed up and down the slope of my rear as it presented itself ready for his touch, lifted high in the air. My breasts were squeezed firmly against the glass, He kept touching, exploring. Then suddenly, he delivered a forceful slap across the plump right cheek. I grimaced and moaned at his first battle cry.

He didn't wait long to continue his erotic corporal attentions. He struck over and over, never hitting one side twice in a row. The heat and friction of his continual spanking penetrated my skin. I could feel the prints of his hands burned onto my now reddened cheeks. It was breathtaking. I stimulated my breasts by pressing and shifting my rock hard nipples back and forth on the cold glass. The tell-tale sign of flooding honey, that always flowed from his touch, ran down my thighs.

With the light pouring in, I knew he'd see my deluge shimmer. He stopped suddenly, confirming my hunch, aware that I was enjoying this too much. As if awestruck by my sudden inundation, he traced his finger along the path of the seeping liquid. He pulled my right leg on the table, leaving me completely open to him. The cleft of my arse spread open, calling for his consideration. He used his crafty tongue to drive me to madness, first licking up some of the juice trickling down my leg. He then followed the forbidden trail to my exposed cleft.

He propelled his clever wet tool up and down the middle of my cheeks, administering bites every few inches, electrifying all the nerve endings that led to my clenching anus. He sucked around it with remorseless fury and I could feel the badges of bruises left by his ferocity. He spread the cheeks of my arse wider in preparation for his lethal impassioned concentrations. He swirled his tongue just outside of the rim and then, around the raised bud. His tongue flicked the puckered skin with carnal exuberance.

As I felt the overwhelming sensations build in my newly exalted region, my body savagely struggled with urgency. He could make me come this way and he knew it too. Unexpectedly, he took both his hands and smacked both my cheeks, once again. He grabbed them in his palms, kneading the scalding warmth as he tongued my quivering hole. His intensity doubled and relentlessly he pierced through the contracting muscles, the gates that kept him from driving home his final act of plunder. I screamed out his name in luscious torment. His tongue jack-hammered my anus, pounding in and out, bringing me one step closer to the point of climax. My mind was clouded, thinking a single thought, '*I'm almost there. Please just fuck it harder and deeper*.' He must have sensed what I needed to bring me right to the edge and he quickly replaced his tongue with a more fulfilling finger. He pumped with deliberate strokes only to abruptly … stop.

I felt his finger retreat from me. Damn it, he must have some other sort of punishment in mind. His jeans rustled as they hit the ground. He pulled me up, whipped me around, and lowered my body until I was on my knees, in supplication to him. My hands tugged against the binding that kept them tied behind my back. I longed to pull free his massive cock from the confines of his boxer shorts. I scooted closer to him. He pushed me down to rest on my heels and barked, 'Don't move.'

I whimpered in protest.

'None of that, Minx. You will have to learn your

lesson first.' I pouted at his reprisal. He swiped his thumb across my lips. 'You do want me to fuck that insatiable arse of yours with my cock, don't you?'

He knew he didn't have to ask. There was no uncertainty or hesitation. I wanted him to take me that way. I wanted beyond all things to be filled by his throbbing gift of mythic proportions. Just the thought of it always made my cunt shudder.

'This is my time and with my time your luscious arse will be filled with our little toy stretching you until you're ready for me to fuck it.'

I shuddered at the thought. His words made my demanding craving all the more unbearable. He hadn't made me come yet and my body screamed in rebellion. Instead of alleviating my torture, he continued to feed its frustration. He pulled through the opening in his boxers to wield a perfect creation of manhood. 'Please,' I gasped. He knew what the plea was for. He knew that I wanted him to fuck my mouth. 'Oh no, this is part of your penalty. You will sit there and watch what you could've had if you'd obeyed me.'

Spreading my knees wide for easy access, he lowered himself down to rub first his balls and then his cock in my folds. I drove my body forward so my cunt would consume what he kept from me. Aware of my skullduggery, he pulled out immediately. 'I told you keep still,' he admonished. His eyes glinted with mischief as he rose. His cock now hung inches from my mouth. He had one hand caressing his balls and the other firmly wrapped around his cock. He slowly teased himself with my lubrication until not one spot was without my wetness.

My mouth opened to an 'O' in mutiny. I had to get

off. My beyond-swollen clit felt like a drum solo, pulsing so hard that every squirm or movement drove me one step closer to coming but never quite let me reach release. As if to infuriate me, he would stop at mid-stroke and smile as if he was pausing to imagine the tight muscles of my anus around it. Then playfully, he'd continue moving his hand up and down the shaft. I tightened my vaginal muscles with fast but steady squeezes like a metronome, hoping that it would help me come.

'How is Pandora doing?' he said with a chuckle, motioning with his eyes to my vibrating cunt at one of his deliberate halts. I gave an agonising lament.

'Do you want to come, Minx?'

'God, yes,' I hissed.

'Maybe I will let you, but first stick your tongue out.' She swiftly obliged. 'Not good enough. More. Ah, that's it.' He placed his tightening balls on my spread tongue while still hand fucking himself. Their welcome heat urged my tongue to sway back and forth on their underside.

'Lick all your cream off. Do it now.' I greedily lapped my juice that covered the globes of tautening skin, which were now filling with his own cum.

'Does it taste good?'

Good? My mind and body rolled with excitement. '*No, not good,*' my eyes told him, *but rather sweet, hot and fucking incredible.*

His movements seemed to accelerate. He backed up a little. 'Now, open wider, yes … that's it, keep your tongue out.' I could tell he was about to come. His face grimaced and his control seemed to falter. His fevered strokes almost brushed my face. 'Now Minx, I'm going to fill your mouth with what should have been in your delicious cunt. With a groan he said, 'I'm going to … come on your tongue so you can taste what will fill your arse, and then you will crave it there every moment.'

When the first shot of his come hit my tongue, he started to lower himself to me. His cock was still unloading as I felt his other hand pinch my clit. While the remaining downpour slipped down my throat, he finger fucked me with his forefinger and middle finger, while his thumb flicked my clit. My release was almost instantaneous. I screamed my orgasm against his inner thigh. He dropped his other hand from his cock and caressed the side of my face. 'Ah Minx, I didn't even have to fuck you with my cock to make you scream. You've learned your lesson haven't you, though?'

I nodded. He untied me and gently lifted me to take me to the bedroom. After he laid me on my bed, passing one long finger across my cheek, he moved a stray hair and hooked it behind my ear. I gazed at him adoringly. He reached inside my nightstand and put our favourite toy in my hand.

'My time is my time and don't ever forget again or else I'll have to come up with another punishment,' he said, smiling broadly as I rubbed his glorious handprint that still left an impression on my backside. Turning me to the side for a better view, he traced the outline of my enflamed skin. He bent down to kiss away the burn and lingered there for a moment, taking in the gorgeous sight. Then silently, he rose to leave. Heading toward the hallway, he turned back when I said boldly, 'A punishment to some, to some a gift, and to many a favour.' A sly amusement washed over his face. For a split second, I could see the waver of want to start our games all over again.

'Virgil?' he asked.

'No, Seneca.'

'Ahh …' he said as he descended the stairs. After hearing the door swing shut, I leaned over and put the toy back in my nightstand. His time was over now. The front door closed without out my protest because I knew he'd be back tomorrow. I whispered with a sated grin, 'Thank you, DH.' I turned to my side and in more than a whisper with a kitty cat stretch, I spoke dreamily, 'Minx, huh? Hmmn …' I shut my eyes and settled in the covers for a well-needed nap.

Backstage
by Roger Frank Selby

'MISS LACEY!'

'Good evening, er …'

'Rod Styles.'

'Ah yes, Mr Styles. Look, I know it's late, but I need to go backstage for five minutes and have a look at the new set for Act Two.'

'Sorry, miss, don't think that would be allowed. I'm responsible for Health and Safety and there's a lot of heavy kit on that set.'

She turned on her smile and took off her coat, revealing a skin-tight sweater beneath. Laura Lacey's stunning figure had played a bigger part than acting ability in landing this leading role, and she knew it. 'You can call me Laura, er, Rod. Mr Erikson asked me to familiarise myself with the set before rehearsals. I'll be very careful, I promise.'

She saw his jaw drop as he took in the full view. He looked as though he would like to familiarise himself with her set.

Eventually he spoke. 'I suppose it will be OK … Laura.'

He let her in, turned the lights full on and followed

her backstage.

She stepped up among the dark timbers and wrought-iron of the massive equipment on the set. She breathed in the pleasant smell of wood, metal, paint; there was also the sharp tang of leather.

'Impressive, ain't they?'

It looked as if he was going to follow her around like a big puppy. 'Why don't you make yourself a coffee, or something, while you wait in your office.' She turned off the smile.

'Oh, right … But be careful; everything works. We don't want you getting hurt now, do we?' he warned her breasts.

After he'd gone, she inspected the equipment. She wasn't sure of the function of some of it. The rack was nastily obvious, of course. She spun the wheel and the loud jangle of chains made her jump.

'You OK out there?' he called out from his office behind the scenes.

'Yes, I'm fine; don't worry.' Jesus, what a pain he was. She turned to the guillotine. My God, that angled blade looked sharp! She had an impulse to kneel down and settle her head into the notch, just for a moment … No. Wisely, she kept her distance.

Ah, this looked more reversible: stocks. A pair of stocks? She wasn't sure of the terminology, but these looked the part – notches in a pair of sturdy planks that formed three holes when brought together – as now. Quite large holes for neck and wrists. They certainly didn't look narrow enough to prevent her slim hands from pulling out. She put her coat down.

She opened the stocks carefully, lifting the hanging hasp aside from its lock-ring, and holding up the top plank, hinged on the right. She settled her neck into the generous central hole, noticing the soft leather padding for the first time. 'How nice!' She was bent over quite deeply by the time her throat rested on the hide.

Putting her right hand in its slot, she found more padding. Getting the left hand located was a little trickier, but she found she could easily take the weight of the top plank on her neck. With her left hand now in position, she lowered her neck. To escape, she had merely to lift her neck again, and …

There was a metallic click as the descending hasp slipped over the locking ring.

'Oh, fuck.'

She resisted the impulse to call for assistance; she could work this out herself. She tried to pull her left hand through, but the snug padding made the hole smaller that it had looked. Damn! There *had* to be a solution that didn't require her calling out that that cocky stage manager.

The out-of-the-box thinking that had helped her pass naval officer selection a few years back went into high gear. There was a toolbox nearby, but just out of range. Then she had the solution. By swinging the whole heavy device from side to side on its stand, the hasp could be made to swing just clear of the loop.

A lift with her neck at the right moment and she was free.

The experience hadn't frightened her, quite the reverse. Bent right over with her round arse all stuck out and vulnerable, had made her feel decidedly frisky. 'Now, Laura, behave yourself! You know where these things can lead.'

Ignoring herself, she crept round to the stage

manager's office and peeped through the glass in a chink between posters.

He wasn't making coffee. He was watching a porn channel! His hand was inside his fly. Fascinated she watched the action. A full-breasted woman was being stripped by two men and carefully tied up. She liked what she saw both on and off screen. A simple scheme took shape in her mind – *just* the sort of thing that had got her cashiered from the Navy. However, conduct unbecoming an actor was not an offence in Civvy Street, as far as she knew.

She had to dash back and prepare, *before* he progressed too far – and she'd told him only five minutes!

'Rod!'

Damn! That stuck-up bitch; what the fuck did she want? – just when the big-titted one was about to get it.

'With you in a mo!' he called, trying to stuff himself back into his trousers. Shit! It wasn't going to go down in time. Instead he tucked the tip of his cock under his belt; his leather jacket would cover his temporary embarrassment.

Arriving at the scene he could hardly believe what he saw. He had to laugh. 'Blimey, what have you gone and done with yourself!' There she was, all nicely ready for him in the stocks. He hadn't really appreciated just how well the low neck-hole could present a woman's body for possible service.

High-heeled shoes set well apart, her long legs reached all the way up to her barely covered arse – and what an arse! And she didn't really seem to mind him seeing so much of it – too bad if she did!

'And how did you get your skirt caught up in the lock like that? You're giving me quite an eyeful, you know, Laura!'

'I'm sorry to be so stupid, Rod. I just couldn't resist trying it out. The skirt was to stop the hasp slipping over that round bit. Instead it seems to have jammed up the whole thing! Look, *do you mind* coming around to the front where I can see you?'

He dragged his eyes away from her lovely behind and did as she asked. 'Yeah, no worries,' he said briskly, taking off his jacket, 'we should be able to free …'

Her mouth dropped open.

'What?'

'Your belt … *Above* your belt!'

'Oh shit! I'm sorry. I …'

This was all going nicely to plan, she thought. 'Rod, that happened a little suddenly, didn't it?'

'Well, I …'

'What *were* you up to when I called you?' She used her teasing voice.

'Nothing … Hey, look, Lady Laura, you're hardly in a position to question me! Surely, I'm allowed to get a little excited with you waving your bare arse at me like that.'

'So now you have your bare … um, member, waving at *me*?'

'It seems that way, don't it?' He looked down with pride.

With them both looking, it grew a little taller – like an extending periscope peeping up for a look. It reminded her of her Navy days. She licked her lips, conveniently at his belt-level. 'And my bottom's not *completely* bare, is it?'

'That could be arranged.'

She was still gazing at the pink periscope. 'Well, let's not get ahead of ourselves … Look, I can see I've been a fool; I *will* do something for you if you just let me out.'

'What?'

'Just step a little closer.'

He did, the round head of his rampant flesh an inch from her pursed lips. The tip of her tongue slowly extended to touch the tip of his cock. He held still while she licked all around the head. A little clear fluid appeared at the top and she licked it off in an instant.

'There. Now let me out.'

He undid his belt and released himself. He stepped out of his jeans and shorts. He was quite splendidly endowed, she thought. 'What are you playing at Rod? – I said let me out, not let *him* out!'

'That wasn't very much, Laura. I'm sure a girl like you could do a lot better than that.'

'OK. Now this is just a little treat, so don't get too carried away, Rod. You'll find a bottle of oil in my handbag down there. If you pour a little in the palm of my left hand … Well, you'll find out what I can do for you.'

If he had any doubts that she'd arranged this, they vanished as he rummaged through her bag and found the oil – sweet edible oil, too. My God, she must have spotted him weeks ago when she first came to the theatre – and he thought she didn't know he existed. His cock felt like it was going to climb right out of his crotch with excitement!

'Here it is, my lovely Laura. Are you going to put it

on for me?'

'Less of the "lovely", Mr Styles. Let's get this over with and then you can release me.'

His disappointment at her attitude must have showed.

'Oh, don't worry, I'll make this very nice for you. Come over to my left and I'll see what I can do with one hand.' She held out her left hand and he poured a little oil into her palm. He saw the look in her eyes as she took in his full erection. She wanted it all right! He had to kneel down a little to allow her to palm the oil over the tip and along the top part of his shaft. Her fingers felt gloriously sexy as they moved up and down the shaft and around the wide helmet.

'Stand a little higher so I can reach down.'

Her fingers now slid right down to the base, and then scooped up his balls. For a moment she gripped him tightly and he wondered if he had miscalculated. 'You seem to have me by the balls, Laura.'

'I do, don't I?'

Then she massaged the oil all around, weighing his fruit, feeling the root of his cock behind them. She began working up the shaft again, and he instinctively lowered her work so she could reach the top. As she cupped his helmet he felt a throb. He was oiled from tip to top, and now a little more spunk was oozing out to join the oil.

'This is very naughty, you taking advantage of me, like this, Rod, but just let me have another a lick of the top, will you?'

Still half kneeling, legs akimbo, he offered it to her mouth. Her lips enveloped the head instantly. He felt her tongue exploring all around him, tasting the oil and him. Her head extended out a little to take in more. He gave her more and more until … God, he must be halfway down her throat! He withdrew a little and began a gentle in and out. She was working frantically with her mouth. It was lovely … Hey – she was trying to make him come!

He pulled out.

'That was sudden.'

'You were trying to finish me off!'

'Was I? Well, you can't blame a girl for trying. Anyway, that's quite enough for now; you can set me free.'

'What!'

'I said I'd do you a small favour, and I have – several, in fact.'

'I've got news for you, my lovely bossy Laura with your big tits and arse. You ain't going nowhere until *I* say so, and we haven't finished yet – not by a long chalk! That surprised you, didn't it? Women like you are always getting their own fucking way when others are around – but not here, tonight, Laura. Do you honestly think I'm going to let you go now, all bent over for me, while you've been getting my dick all ready for fucking?'

'Look Rod, I'm not in a good negotiating position right now, so do what you need to do. You sound a little angry about a type of woman. I'm not really that type, but get it out of your system with me. I don't mind if … if you spank me a little. In fact I might enjoy that.'

He could hardly believe it. She *had* set this up! Fighting down his urgent desire, he tried to keep his voice stern: 'So you like a little spanking do you

Laura? Have you been a naughty girl?'

'Well, yes … Yes, I certainly *have*, Mr Styles.'

'Good, a bit more respect now, I see. I'm glad we understand each other. If you behave yourself and do as you are told you'll be OK. Now let's have a look at that hasp.' He pulled away the twist of skirt where it had tangled. There was a ripping of cloth. He tore the material right off her waist and threw it aside. 'Well you won't be needing that skirt, and just to make sure you are *nicely* secure …' He fetched a hefty padlock from the toolbox, slotted it through the locking ring projecting through the hasp and snapped it shut.

'Now let's see what you have on offer, Miss Lacey.'

He collected a pair of shears from the toolbox and went round behind her. 'My, you are a big girl! Where shall we start? Let's feel those knockers you like 'like to flash around – see if they're real.' He grabbed her left breast and fondled it roughly for a moment. 'Lovely! Now let's have a look.' He lifted her clothes up her back, exposing her bra-strap. 'I won't be able to undress you with your head and arms through that board, so we are going to have to snip a little. Is that OK?'

She hesitated. 'Please be careful of my body, Mr Styles.'

He was careful. He didn't want to mark that smooth, lilywhite skin of hers. He ran the shears up the back of her sweater, snipping all the way to her neck. Then he snipped across each shoulder and down each sleeve to the wrist. Clearing the spoiled clothing away, he uncovered a nice expanse of smooth back, bisected by her black brassiere strap. 'And now the bra.' Three snips – and it should have fallen to the floor. He looked underneath. The silky cups, double-D maybe, still clung to the white globes of her boobs while the cut straps dangled. Suction, probably. He pulled each cup off, revealing pointed nipples, brown cones upon the milky breast-flesh – just how he liked them.

'Wow, Laura! What superb tits you have.' He grabbed and squeezed them as they hung down. 'Real, natural ones, with lovely stand-up nipples to bite!'

He played around under her for a while, sucking and biting close up to the puckering flesh. Apart from the odd ouch and groan as he nibbled, sucked and fondled her breasts, she was silent. She seemed to be enjoying it, but probably wouldn't admit it.

'Is that nice? Do you like me playing with your big tits like this?' He squeezed and kneaded her deeply as he waited for her answer.

'Ah … If I say I'm enjoying it, Mr Styles, will you, Ahh … let me go?

'Not yet Laura, I haven't quite finished with you yet.'

Nor have I with you, she thought. You have a tiger by the tail, my sporty stage manager. Rod the Rod really knew how to handle her body, but he was too sure of himself in his impositions.

While he still hefted the weight of her left breast in a warm hand, she felt his other hand gently stroking her raised bottom. She let her buttocks roll beneath the lace panties as she shifted her weight a little. Then he slipped his hand under the waistband, against her skin, and moved smoothly over the roundness of her right cheek, fingers slipping into the crevasse just above her anus. He eased the lace down over her cheeks and thighs. Her pussy must now be exposed to him – it was so wet it felt cold!

'Step out of your knickers and open your legs a bit more.' She did, and went astride for him, her bottom fully bared.

Smack!

Not quite hard enough, she thought, but the exploratory spank had made her catch her breath. She felt her heart beating a little faster.

'Mr Styles?'

'Yes Laura?'

'I have been *quite* a bad girl.'

'Right!'

Smack!

'Ow!'

His open hand smacked her satisfyingly hard on the right buttock cheek – then gripped it, killing the slight wobble. Her little spontaneous yelp was just about right, she thought, informing him that the spanking was not too hard. She felt her bottom clench a little in anticipation. Her heart was racing.

Smack!

'Ow!'

He did the same on her left side. He repeated the double spank and grip maybe a dozen times. She particularly enjoyed the powerful buttock squeeze that followed each smack.

Then he placed both hands on her tingling bottom – surely glowing a little red – and briskly shimmied her cheeks around until she felt her breast wobbling in sympathy. She felt ready to be taken.

'Hey! What are you doing?'

He'd picked up her left ankle. She had to balance on her right leg as he lifted it higher and higher, hooking it through a loop of rope dangling from the scenery. Her shoe fell off with a clatter. 'Just opening you up a little more, Laura.'

With one leg high in the air, her whole body was twisted to the left. His hands touched and swung her breasts at this new angle, which certainly had her much more open to him in every way. Then, starting with both hands around her high ankle, he ran his touch all the way down her raised leg until he was holding the inside and outside of her thigh at the groin.

She felt him cup her opened box. She was dripping wet.

She felt a shock and a tingle as his fingers went up inside her. Her spasm around his fingers caused her to hop around a little to keep her balance. His hand slipped in deeper with the movement.

Rod was good with his fingers. He soon had her moaning as he fingered her folds and probed her.

Then she felt his naked hip rough against her belly. Her lifted thigh was now pressed against his T-shirt as he embraced it. Her single standing leg felt *his* legs either side. He was going to play scissors with her! His fingers came out of her to guide his weapon in.

'I can't wait any longer, Laura!'

Neither could she.

Legs vertically astride like a ballerina, she was already wide open, and at last he slid his cock fully up inside her. It slipped in with little forcing, thanks to the angle and the oiling she'd supplied. She let out a deep sigh as he filled her. Then he moved slowly in and out, feeling the ripple of inner muscles as she shifted her balance.

'Is that, ah, different for you, Laura?' he gasped.

'Has anyone, fucked you like this before?'

'Not *exactly* like this, ah no. It's lovely, but it's bloody awkward standing on one leg with your head in the stocks. Hurry up for Christ's sake!'

That made him laugh. Still deep inside her he reached up and slipped her foot from the rope. Lowering her leg slowly, her bottom pivoted around his axis in a very satisfying way, as he shifted from her side to directly behind her.

With her foot fully on the floor, her bottom angled a little without her shoe, she still pushed nicely up against him.

'How's that, now?'

'Ah, that's *much* better,' she sighed.

For quite a while he simply fucked her with slow, deep strokes, holding onto her wide, cream-smooth bottom as it moved majestically beneath his hands. But the pressure was gathering rapidly inside him and the tickle of her cervix at her full depth was going to set him off soon.

He wanted to make it last. But her muscles were beginning to contract around him. Her vagina felt like a gloved hand running up and down his length as he slid in and out.

And then her motion shifted up a gear. Her bottom tossed and rolled while holding him in its grip. He felt as helpless as a raft in mountainous seas, just holding on as she began to howl. He was going to blow any second …

He let go and exploded into her. The come lasted as he thrust and slapped hard against her bottom, holding on tightly, crying out to match her howls as he repeatedly spurted into her.

Finally he was spent. She felt him pull out and the warmth seep down her inner thighs … But then he went round to her head and gloated. 'Now my lovely well-fucked Laura, what am I going to do with you now? You realise I can do what I like with you until you beg to be released?'

She was so disappointed in him. There was no need for this. In a generous mood after that quite adequate screwing, she would give him a final chance to redeem himself. 'Nonsense! I rather enjoyed all that. You made me come beautifully, Rod. Don't you realise I set up the whole situation? Now, don't be a silly arse, release me right now, and we'll do it again tomorrow evening. I really *mean* that, but it's my final offer.'

He laughed. 'As you said, Laura, you're not in a good negotiating position! *No*. Not until I decide.'

The office phone rang.

'I have to get that. Be back in a jiffy. Don't run away now!' he laughed.

When he was out of sight, she lifted her neck and right wrist together, raising the top plank. It pivoted on the padlocked end – lifting free where she had previously removed the lower screws from the hinge.

She collected her shoe and panties from the stage, and grabbed her coat – it wouldn't be the first time she'd go home wearing nothing under it.

She walked stark naked around to the office and cracked open the door. He was still on the phone. She opened the door fully.

He looked up sharply. His face was a picture, shifting through ludicrous expressions of surprise, dismay – and disappointment as she slowly and luxuriously put her coat on and closed off the view.

He covered the mouthpiece. 'I suppose … tomorrow …?

'In your dreams. Goodbye, Mr Styles.'

She blew him a kiss and left.

Happy Birthday Ben
by Roxanne Sinclair

THE SEAM ON THE front of Helen's unlined coat caught her nipple as she walked. With nothing but fresh air between them the ridge of stitching was free to tantalise her with every step that she took. Helen smiled and enjoyed the sensation.

The August day was warm and the coat was enough to protect her modesty as she sashayed her way through the park.

Someone called her name and she turned around. She raised her hand and waved to the four guys who were working on flower beds near the tennis courts. They were Ben's workmates. As she waved the belt around her waist loosened and the front of her coat fell apart slightly exposing her cleavage.

There was no one around and Helen left the coat as it was. The breeze felt good as it brushed her breasts.

She moved the basket that she was carrying from one hand to the other. As she moved it across the front of her she allowed the rigid handle to catch the fabric and pull it apart. With her pubic area exposed, if only briefly, Helen tingled with excitement and anticipation.

With the moistness increasing between her legs

Helen was tempted to run but she forced herself to walk slowly. Her knowledge of what was coming heightened her growing pleasure with every step she took.

When she'd told Ben that she would bring him lunch on his birthday he'd told her to meet him in the shed at the top of the hill where the tools were stored. It was now five past one so she knew that he would be waiting. He had no idea what he was waiting for.

The shed came into view but still Helen did not quicken her step. Instead she moved the basket across her body again, this time allowing the handle to press into her exposed mound.

She walked purposefully up to the door and stopped in front of it. She allowed her hand to rest on the metal latch for a second and found that it was cold in spite of the warm temperature.

Helen had to exert a little force to move the latch downwards and she opened the door slowly. She put her head around the door and gave her eyes a few seconds to grow accustomed to the dimness.

Ben had his back to her as he worked on a piece of machinery that sat on a bench. The muscles across his back were sculptured under the T-shirt that sweat had stuck to his back.

It was a few moments before Ben put down the tool in his hand and turned around slowly.

'Hi,' he said. The twinkle in his eye was like a star on a dark night.

'Hi,' Helen said with a giggle.

They eyed each other the way they had a thousand times before.

'This is a treat,' Ben said as he wiped his hands on a

cloth, throwing it on a bench.

Helen put the basket on a handy shelf and backed slowly to the door without taking her eyes from Ben's. He looked puzzled and that only added to her growing pleasure.

Sensing the door behind her she reached out and picked up the brush that rested against the wall. She turned around and slid the long handle of the brush through the handles of the door.

'What's going on?' She heard Ben's voice but she did not acknowledge it. Instead, she worked each button in turn until her coat was open. With her back to him she shrugged it off in a couple of movements of her shoulders until it fell at her feet.

She gave Ben a few seconds to admire the view before using her heel to pivot. When she saw Ben's face again it was wearing a huge smile and his eyes were moving up and down the full length of her naked body.

It was a full minute before their eyes met again.

'Happy Birthday Ben.'

His smile widened with every step that she took towards him. Maybe it was the coolness of the shed or maybe it was the fact that she was naked in front of a man she was going to shag that made her breasts pucker up and her nipples stand end. Whatever it was, it felt fantastic.

Helen stopped with her toes inches from Ben's. She looked deep into his eyes and defied him not to ravish her. Her lips were parted slightly and the tip of her tongue was visible between her teeth. Ben closed his eyes slowly, held them there for a few seconds and then opened them again. He thought he was dreaming.

But he wasn't, so Ben moved forward and attached his lips to hers. The first kiss was brief, the second slightly longer and the third deep and passionate. Their open lips massaged each others and after few seconds Ben's tongue slipped out in search of Helen's.

Ben's hands rested on Helen's hips as she pulled his T-shirt from his jeans. Once it was free she put her hands under it and brushed the muscles on his side and back.

She pushed him away from her so that she could peel the shirt from his body. He obliged by lifting his arms above his head and allowing her to free him of the garment which she swung around her head before tossing aside.

Ben circled his arms around Helen and pulled her close to him. His groan of delight as Helen's breast were squashed against his chest was muffled as he buried his face into her neck. He traced the length of her neck with tiny kisses, and then moved along her jaw line before searching out her mouth again.

Now it was Helen's turn to moan as Ben's hand moved to her breast and cupped it gently. He moved his hand in a circular motion, gently at first then harder and faster. She moaned again, longer and louder this time.

'Like that do you?' Ben asked.

'You know I do.'

'You'll like this more,' he assured her as he lowered his head and took the whole of the nipple and surrounding area into his mouth. He held the nipple between his teeth and flicked it with his tongue. Then he stopped flicking and started sucking, gently at first and then ferociously.

Helen threw her head back and took in a deep breath. She laced her fingers in Ben's hair and buried her nails into his scalp.

He loosened his mouth's grip on the breast but kept hold of the nipple with his teeth. He dropped to his knees, letting go of the nipple only after he had stretched it a little.

On his knees his face was inches from her pussy. He looked at it and Helen watched him as he looked at it. Him looking at it was enough to send the tingle that had been lurking around the edges deep inside her.

Helen reached back for the bench that she knew was there. Once located, she took two small steps backwards until she was leaning against it. The chipped edges of the wood felt rough against her bare skin but that only increased the pleasure that was forming between her legs.

With her weight steadied against the bench Helen shuffled her feet so that her legs parted slightly.

This was all the invitation that Ben needed and he fell forward, burying his face into the extended 'V' at the top of her legs. He breathed in deeply, taking in her fragrance.

Then with a practised movement Ben parted the lips between her legs and exposed her excited clitoris. He flicked his tongue over its length. He repeated the motion over and over until soon, Helen was groaning with delight.

As Ben held her lips apart, his thumbs found her hole and worked it.

'Oh my God,' Helen groaned. She lifted herself onto the edge of the bench which allowed her to spread her legs further.

Ben pulled her lips further apart and ran his teeth along her clit.

Her orgasm exploded in his mouth and he sucked her juices dry.

Ben wiped his mouth with the back of his hand before pushing himself to his feet. He stood back and admired her. She had placed her hands behind her back and she was resting on them. Her legs were still wide apart.

She watched Ben's hands work his belt free from the loops around the top of his jeans. He moved slowly and deliberately. She didn't take her eyes from his hands as they worked the buttons of his jeans. Ben lowered his jeans and his boxer shorts together. He stepped out of his boots and kicked his clothes aside with a couple of easy movements.

Helen took in his naked body, allowing her eyes to rest on his cock which seemed, from her perspective, even bigger than its usual eight inches.

He watched her slide from her perch and move slowly to the basket she had brought with her. She stared at his cock the whole time, dragging her eyes from it only at the last second to allow herself to find what she wanted from the basket.

She pulled out a chocolate éclair. She looked from it back to Ben's cock then back to the éclair. She smiled as she licked cream from the end of the cake.

Their eyes were locked together as she walked slowly towards him. Helen opened her mouth and wrapped it around the éclair which she moved in and out of her mouth without taking a bite.

Ben's eyes stared off into the distance as Helen lowered herself to his knees. He didn't need to see what she was going to do to know that he was going to enjoy it.

Helen watched his knob twitch with anticipation.

She separated the éclair. One side had no cream on it and she discarded it immediately. She rubbed the other side against the length of his cock leaving cream in its wake.

She used most of the cream along the shaft before leaving the last blob on his balls.

She twisted herself into a lower position to eat that cream first. She took the whole testicle in her mouth and sucked, gently at first then harder as if she were trying to free the ball from its sac.

His second bollock had had no cream on it but she gave it the same attention.

Then she moved onto the cream that was on his rock-hard stalk. As she licked the cream away the throbbing veins along its length were exposed. She licked and nibbled her way along its entire length, cupping his balls and squeezing as she did so.

When all that remained of the cream was the dollop on his knob-end Helen wrapped her lips around it.

She lowered her head and took as much of it in her mouth as she could. She wrapped her tongue around it and used the muscled in her mouth to tighten her grip. She sucked and nibbled for a couple of minutes until she tasted the first salty drops of spunk.

Ben pulled gently on Helen's hair to stop her work. With his cock resting between her teeth she looked at him.

'Get back on the bench,' he said.

As she released it, Ben's cock slapped back against his stomach.

Helen stood up and did as Ben had told her, moving slowly to give him chance to admire her arse as she walked.

She thought briefly about bending over the bench but changed her mind and climbed onto it. She pushed herself to its edge and spread her legs in open invitation.

Ben moved towards her slowly and stood between her legs. He took his cock in his hand and forced it down. He ran it along the length of her crack a couple of times before allowing it to rest at the edge of her hole. He put his hands on the bench either side of Helen's hips. Their faces were close and their eyes intense.

Ben moved his weight onto his hands and drilled into her. Helen's eyes closed as her pussy stretched around Ben's knob. He moved his hips back until all that remained inside her was his tip. Then he moved forward again slowly until his whole shaft was buried.

He repeated the slow movement a few more times before gradually increasing his speed. He thrust his full length into her each time and Helen threw her head back in delight. She made a guttural noise each time he filled her.

Unable to support the weight Helen dropped back until she was lying flat on the bench.

Ben focused on Helen's breasts which bounced up and down with each of his thrusts.

Those thrusts became quicker and deeper with each movement and their groins ground against each other.

With one final thrust and an animal noise Ben filled Helen.

Minutes later as she let herself out of the shed Helen

enjoyed the feeling of Ben's juices still inside her. As she turned from him and walked away she could feel them trickling down her leg.

She smiled as she waved to the four guys who were still tending the flower beds.

My Cousin's 21st
by Eva Hore

IT WAS MY COUSIN'S 21st and a whole lot of us were crashing at her place overnight in her family room. No drink driving … all we had to do was supply our own bedding.

I'd met a guy who asked if he could share my duvet he hadn't brought his own. He was cute so I thought why not.

'Hey,' someone complained as we accidentally stumbled over them.

'Oops, sorry,' I giggled, a little bit tiddly.

'Be quiet,' someone else hissed.

Still clothed he snuggled up behind me.

Turning my head, I put my mouth to his ear, 'Do you want to fool around?' I whispered.

'Hmm,' he murmured as his hand stole up my skimpy top and over my midriff.

I pushed my arse back into his groin pleased when I felt the distinct hardness of his cock as I wiggled around.

His fingers slipped under my bra where he massaged my breasts before flipping it upwards, exposing my nipples and giving them a good squeeze.

They hardened instantly and he murmured his approval.

I rolled towards him, my hands fumbling with his belt. Quietly, I undid his zip and my hand stole into his jocks. I found a hard, throbbing cock that was responding well to my touch. Inching my fingers inside I eagerly pulled him out. It sprung forward with a mind of its own and I grabbed at his shaft marvelling at its girth while it pulsated in my palm.

I was wishing we were alone somewhere so I could see it as it certainly felt impressive.

Meanwhile Peter had inched up my skirt and his fingers were fumbling with my G-string desperate to get inside. When his fingers brushed against my pubes and down to my slit it was as though an electrical current scorched me and I pulled back involuntarily.

Startled by my reaction he went to remove his hand and accidentally tore my G-string off me, the flimsy material making a loud enough noise in the now quiet room.

We both froze, but everyone must have been sleeping as no comments were forthcoming. Not wanting him to think I was chickening out I grabbed hold of his shaft and began to pump my hand up and down it in slow firm movements. His fingers slid back towards my now naked pussy where he roamed about between my folds before slipping his fingers straight into my cunt.

'Oh man,' he breathed. 'You're so wet.'

'That's so beautiful,' I whispered as he began to finger me.

I wanted to rip my clothing off, straddle him and fuck his brains out but with all these people sleeping up here it was impossible. His fingers were everywhere, roaming around my folds, inside my pussy, slipping up the crack of my arse, twiddling with my puckered hole.

Finally he located my clit, I lifted one leg up, giving him better access, and like a pro he brought me to one of the best orgasms I've ever had while I pumped his shaft furiously.

As my juices exploded out of me I decided if I couldn't fuck him then I'd suck him off. His saturated hand pulled away from me and I could feel my juices everywhere, dribbling down over the inside of my thighs. He brought his hand up to my mouth and I sucked greedily enjoying the taste of myself.

I crushed my mouth to his, my hand still pumping his shaft, my tongue thrusting inside his mouth until I could take no more. I wanted to scream, needed to scream when his hand found my clit again and within seconds I came in the most earth-shattering climax as my body spasmed and shook.

I was desperate for a good fucking but as that was not to be I wiggled back away from him, carefully burying myself down into his groin. I wanted to give him as much pleasure as he'd just given me.

With my bare arse poking out from beneath the duvet I set about swallowing him, my mouth gliding over his massive knob, licking crazily at the pre come which was oozing out of his slit. Then opening my mouth wide, I swallowed carefully right down to the base of his shaft.

Unfortunately his cock hit the back of my throat and I gagged on reflex, pulling back to lick his shaft while catching my breath. He let out a soft moan and I continued, smiling to myself, knowing how good I was at giving head and delighting in the fact that this would be a night he'd never forget.

Now as I sucked him back in, deep into my throat, I felt hands on my arse, fondling me. At first I assumed they were Peter's but then I knew they couldn't be as his hands were groping my breast and holding my head. Pleasantly surprised I wondered if he knew, if he could tell that someone else was joining in.

So instead of being outraged I was excited at the prospect of being involved in a minor threesome. Hands fondling me wasn't as good as a cock but it sure beat nothing. With renewed vigour I sucked harder and then I almost choked when I felt a knob probing my pussy.

I wiggled back harder, encouraging this cock to go further, to open my pussy lips and slide straight in. I wasn't disappointed. Within seconds this unknown cock was slipping and sliding, gliding in and out at a maddeningly slow pace.

I pushed my arse back harder, indicating I wanted more, and I did. It had always been a fantasy of mine to be fucked while sucking some guy's cock and to have it happen here, without planning, well, it was an added bonus.

Never in my wildest dreams would I have thought that this could happen to me. Now my fingers were digging into Peter's groin while I sucked harder, deeper, my tongue slipping around inside my mouth tantalising him while I began to get a faint rhythm going with the cock, neither of us seeming to want to alert Peter to what was happening.

I knew I was on the verge of coming and so was

Peter so I pumped my mouth over his cock wildly hoping the guy fucking me would keep on going. He did. So within seconds I came, gushing around his cock, while Peter exploded down my throat.

As soon as my hot juices poured over this guy's cock I heard a faint murmur of approval and he too came in gallons, his spunk mixing with mine as he shot up high in me.

He pulled his saturated cock out of my pussy and wet my puckered hole with his knob. I tensed, never having had it up the arse before, but all he did was rub my bum with his hand affectionately before pushing his fingers in and out of my pussy, smearing my juices everywhere before leaving me alone.

I snuggled up against Peter, dying for morning to come so I could see the face of the guy who owned the unknown cock, hoping I'd be pleasantly pleased.

High Tea in Suburbia
by Mark Farley

I HAVE THIS FRIEND. Her name is Kim. I see her once a week on a Tuesday evening, in the couple of hours between her book club meeting and her husband arriving home.

Her husband knows all about me. She told him quite recently.

She is a good fifteen to twenty years older than me, and I'm thirty. She is tall and demure, blonde hair, ample bosom, simple hips and a curvy bottom. You know those women who hold themselves like they went to school with one of the Mitford sisters and wear it like a badge? Well, that's how Kim is. Prim, polite and asking the vicar if he would like more tea.

Time has also been good to her for a near fifty-year-old too, despite what she calls 'life's collateral damage' in reference to the excess skin she has collected over the years from giving birth to her three children. She has warned me that a similar fate will eventually befall me, although, without certain advances in medical science, I am not sure how that will happen.

I met her about a year ago. I remember it well.

It was at this high-end deli called Ottolenghi on Ledbury Road, in that affluent part of West London suburbia I walk through on my way to work. In fact, it's still our private little joke when we see each other. Now, during those awkward pauses when we're getting dressed we think back and laugh about how we peppered each other with curious glances over the bowls of sautéed peppers, mushrooms and thirty different types of potato salad.

As I stepped out onto the leafy residential avenue moments later to rummage through the embossed paper bag for my over-priced sandwich, I noticed that Kim was at sixes and sevens with the basket on the front of her traditional Pashley Princess bicycle. She fiddled with the chain lock before stuffing it into the wicker basin over the front wheel and putting on her helmet.

She saw me and again we exchanged smiles and I decided to wait before setting off to Portobello.

She looked as if she was about to pedal away but then glanced at me once more. I nodded and rolled my eyes in a very naughty way. She looked away haughtily and started to rotate the pedals. I thought fast. There was only one thing I could think of to say.

"I'll race you, if you like." I chuckled, realising that I was giving her the opportunity to make me look like a right idiot just by pushing off and leaving me behind on the pavement.

I am sure this crossed her mind too, as she paused with a hint of a smile on her face.

"Where would you race me to?" she asked, warming to my cheeky charm, I hoped.

"Anywhere," I replied. She looked slightly alarmed,

perhaps she realised she was being chatted up, possibly for the first time in years. She glanced me up and down, in what I am convinced was wonderment.

"Oh dear," I thought. "You've gone too far this time." She was wearing that expression that said 'God, you're young enough to be my son'.

She sighed and looked around for anyone she knew. The coast was clear, so she signalled for me to join her. We walked, as she pushed her bicycle, to an outlet of a coffee chain on Westbourne Grove. As I queued and ordered lattes, Kim chained her bike to a lamppost and found a table. I turned with my hands full and noticed her sitting bolt upright and felt a bit guilty about the lascivious thoughts swirling around my head.

Why would a woman like her want me, I pondered? Or was she just being polite?

My lust, fuelled by my long-standing penchant for older women, was not deterred though, as I admired her in her light, flowery summer dress and white tennis shoes. I saw that she held her knees together and had her hands placed demurely on her lap.

The conversation soon turned to those thoughts in my head. She didn't mess about and clearly wanted to get down to brass tacks. She started to berate me even before the head of my posh coffee had been disturbed.

"I hope you realise that I have absolutely no plans to let you fuck me."

I paused, hot beverage in mouth. I smiled. I was ever so slightly flattered that she had at least thought about it, but I was worried about the twitching ears of the people at the neighbouring tables.

"I hadn't asked." I said quietly. "Yet."

"Well, don't be getting any of those ideas, young

man, because I am a happily married woman …" she nodded to herself in agreement.

"Right then." I sipped at my coffee with a defeated sigh. We glanced at each other as we returned our cups to their saucers and leaned back in our chairs.

"So why did you come then?" I asked her. Her eyebrows rose as she contemplated her answer.

"You intrigue me, and one assumes that considering your boldness … enough to almost proposition a woman, particularly someone like me, in the street like you did, you are a man who likes to dominate …?"

"Well, err …"

"I take it you like to spank your women too?"

"Actually, no. I'm more of a submissive. I'm sorry."

"Sorry …?" she bellowed with a hearty bray, before leaning forward towards me and patting my thigh. "Oh darling, don't be sorry. We're going to get on splendidly."

"Earl Grey, OK?" she said , as she dropped her keys next to a bowl of potpourri on her hall table. She untangled herself from the pashmina around her shoulders and I ran my eyes across her bare shoulders and over her breasts. My chest started to pound.

I was surprised how the snug, almost cottage-like terrace opened up from the inside. I hadn't realised that places like this existed. I walk past houses like this every day, without even a thought of what might be inside. I stepped back towards the front door; an oak door to my right was ajar and through it I could make out a piano in the vast room beyond. I walked over to it and saw some Mozart sheet music open and some scribbling and alterations made on it.

She ushered me into the kitchen and seated me at a recently stripped wooden table. I had an urge to flick through the open newspaper but thought twice when I realised it was the Daily Mail.

"What do you do?"

"Me? I work in this bookshop and I write. I'd love to be able to do it all the time but bills have to be paid, you know?"

"My son is a freelance journalist. I hear all about it."

"Tell me about your husband," I enquired.

"George is a brilliant man. He's in the city. Hedge funds. Wastes his life down there. I'll be so glad when he finally hangs up that tie and briefcase and we can actually get on with our marriage."

I nodded, slightly distracted.

"The thing is that he's a terrible fuddy-duddy. Always has been. Think it's the Oxford in him personally. If we had met over in Cambers, I might have been able to bring out his wilder side."

I tried to laugh, but it really was another world to me.

"What I am trying to say is that he doesn't fulfil me sexually. You understand?"

My ears pricked up and she had my full attention.

"The sex always dies after a while though …" I sympathised.

"No, that's not what I mean."

I had already guessed what this was all about. I was just being polite really.

"He won't let you spank him?"

"Exactly my dear. Or vice versa, which I don't mind

myself. Honestly though, you hear all these stories from professional mistresses about how all their clients are captains of industry and company executives and love having the power taken away from them, whereas mine is not all interested in giving his wife a little pain for pleasure."

She continued to talk to me as she moved back to the boiling kettle. I watched her as she kicked off her shoes, her dainty feet leaving the slight impression of bare soles on the tiled floor. I stared at the floor as she poured the water. She wiped her brow. The sweat marks on the floor soon disappeared and the submissive in me wanted to search for her scent trail on my hands and knees. I wondered what it would be like to smell of her.

"What is it?" she snapped, as I drifted off into a reverie.

"You have lovely feet …"

"A foot man, huh?"

"Uh-huh." I nodded, our eyes locked together. She carried over the tea tray and smiled wickedly to herself.

"I knew it. I could tell. My last plaything was a foot lover. Do you want to know what I made him do?"

I nodded respectfully. She took a ceramic pot and placed it in front of me. She arranged the cups and saucers meticulously between us. The milk, the sugar bowl. They were all correct and, I imagined, just how they should be laid out. There were ginger biscuits arranged neatly on a side plate. I could already smell the infusion of bergamot as she wagged her finger at me, beckoning me as she backed away from the table.

She stopped in the middle of the kitchen floor, the

exact part of the floor she had just crossed when I noticed her feet. I stood facing her, towering over her.

"Strip …" she demanded. "Everything."

I needed no more encouragement. A beautiful and smart older woman putting me in my place. She leaned back onto the black marble counter behind her and watched me undress until I stood before her, naked as the day I was born.

"Wonderful boy …" she grinned as she took in what I had. "Now kneel …"

I obliged.

She held out her leg and pointed her foot, not unlike a ballerina. She ran her toe up my chest and the lines of my neck, to my ear and then it hovered over my mouth. I turned slightly and put out my tongue for her.

"Nah ha ha," she gasped. "Not yet. You're mine to play with."

I closed my mouth obediently, and let her continue. The sole of her foot pressed against my lips and I was treated to a toenail tickling one of my nostrils. The scent of her, her very being, filled my senses and I devoured the taste. She rubbed the ball of her foot into my nose and over one eye before scratching down the middle of my chest, stopping at my crotch. My legs parted for her and she started to bat playfully at my balls. She continued to lean back on the counter and demanded I should lean back on the floor behind me so she had a full view of me. She lifted the front of her skirt and rubbed her crotch as she continued to knead my flaccid cock with her toes.

She placed her foot on my chest and pushed me back until I was flat on my back and looking up at the ceiling. Again with her foot in my face, she instructed me to open my eyes and watch her masturbate. I had a view right up her skirt and to her ugly grey panties. I could see that she was enjoying my looking at her. That was enough for me to harden down below. She commented on it.

"My, what a gifted young man you are."

I laughed, not feeling in any way uncomfortable. She purred delicately. She held her sole to my closed mouth for me to savour and rubbed away gently at herself with two lean fingers until she was satisfied.

She walked over to the table and poured herself a cup of the Earl Grey.

"Okay, down there?" she directed her question to where I was still lying beneath her.

"Yes, absolutely." Actually I was reminded of my state by a draught from the hallway.

"Good, go to my room. I'm just getting started."

I clambered to my feet, as she rummaged in the drawer of a nearby dresser.

"… and take this. I may have a use for it."

She handed me a long wooden ruler, the kind she probably used years ago at school.

"Hmmm, I like the look of this …"

She sipped at the porcelain cup.

"You won't be doing much looking at it. But you will be feeling it soon."

I grinned, happy that I had found a kindred spirit.

"Go, top of the stairs, second door on the right." she ordered. "I will join you when I have had my tea and finished reading the paper."

She turned away from me and took a seat, her back still straight.

I scurried away obediently.

Spring Break Girls
Hot Sun, Sand, Surf, And S-E-X
by Lynn Lake

SPRING BREAK, THAT ONE-WEEK mid-March holiday when kids young and old break free of the snow and cold to soak up some hot sun, warm waves, cool drinks, and good times on faraway beaches. A pleasant vacation for parents and their children, a rowdy party for high school and college kids. And for many barely legal beauties burgeoning into sweet womanhood, a rite of passage into the very grown-up world of sexual pleasure.

As a travel agent, I've put together literally thousands of Spring Break getaway packages for my clients, including many for giggly, gushing girls just turned that most glorious of all ages – eighteen. They're young and anxious for fun in the sun; an escape from the drudgery of dorm life and study halls; a chance to experience new and wild things far removed from normal parental controls and school and community standards. But as I've found out time and again, what happens on Spring Break doesn't always stay at that Spring Break destination.

Most of my clients are repeat customers, and since

bubbly young women just *can't* keep a secret, I often get to hear all about their previous Spring Break adventures when I'm booking their next escapade. I get good feedback on the accommodations, restaurants, and entertainment packages, of course, but I also get sizzling bonus commentary on what went down when the girls went wild.

From frantic first-time groping on the sun-baked white sands of Pensacola Beach, to all-out girl-on-girl foam party dancing into the wee small hours of a Mazatlan morning, I've heard it all. And broken down by the current hottest Spring Break destinations, are just some of those tales of teen girl travel lust.

Cancun, Mexico

Located at the tip of the Yucatan Peninsula, this 13-mile-long sunshine island offers just about everything for the dedicated tourist and party animal alike: wide, sugary beaches; warm, turquoise Caribbean waters; exotic nightclubs by the dozen; and even historically significant Mayan ruins. There're plenty of watersports to choose from, of course, and a wide variety of beach games, like volleyball and soccer, bikini contests, limbo dancing and salsa wrestling. But what got one client of mine, Emma, all tingly with excitement was the infamous Cancun 'booze cruise' – the party boat ride over to Isla Mujeres.

'I guess I had, like, maybe, one or two drinks,' the brunette cutie concedes.

Dressed in her sober school uniform – simple white blouse and blue plaid skirt, white stockings and black shoes – it's hard to even imagine the hard stuff passing between the petite, pigtailed eighteen-year-old's lips.

But harder stuff than tequila passed between those kewpie-doll lips, it seems.

'It was my first blowjob ever!' she enthuses. 'And I think I did pretty good at it.'

I ask her to collect her thoughts, get them in order, and she nods.

'Okay, I was on the boat, right, and everyone was drinking and dancing and stuff, having a really good time, right. And I guess I got kinda carried away – with, like, a total stranger!'

It seems young Emma got separated from her high school friends and ended up in the touchy, feely arms of a college boy five years her senior, on the one part of the boat not swarming with humanity – a storage locker below-decks.

'It was all full of life jackets and gasoline cans and yucky junk like that. It wasn't very romantic, that's for sure. But we made out for a while anyway, kissing and frenching and stuff. Until Brad sorta pushed me down – you know, down to my knees.'

Emma pauses, her pretty face flushing red.

'He wanted me to, you know, suck his … thing,' she finally continues, looking up at me with her shy violet eyes. 'I know, 'cause he pulled his shorts down and his … thing popped out and kinda slapped my chin.'

'Had you ever performed fellatio before?'

'Nope. But I was in a performance of Othello once.' Emma laughs at her joke, then quickly turns serious again. 'I'd never even seen a … cock before that night – in person, anyway. And I didn't see it any too good that night, either, 'cause it was so dark and stuff. But I sure did feel it.'

Emma admits to liking the feel of Brad's big, hard cock in her small, sweaty hand, the grunts of pleasure she drew out of her fellow traveller by moving her hand up and down his shaft.

'He was all, like, 'Suck it! Suck it!' So I opened my mouth and he stuck it right inside. It was pretty weird having the thing, like, half-buried in my mouth. It was all hot and hard, and I could feel it, like, throbbing. Feel it all the way down to my cunny, you know. Anyway, I kinda bobbed my head up and down, sucking on it, right.'

The fresh-faced teen worries her pleated skirt with her gloss-tipped fingers, then says, 'I probably actually scraped it more than sucked it, but I must've done something right, 'cause Brad grabbed my pigtails and pumped his hips and groaned like he was really enjoying himself. He even smacked the back of my throat a couple of times, and I hardly gagged at all,' she brags. 'But then he really started jerking around, and my mouth filled up with this warm, salty stuff – his, uh, cum, right.'

'Did you swallow?'

'Ewww! Are you kidding!?' Emma frowns. 'I just, like, rubbed him with my hand and he sprayed all over my face.' She smiles contentedly. 'He seemed pretty happy with that.'

Daytona Beach, Florida

With 23 miles of hot, ocean-lapped beach and loads of attractions like Disney World, SeaWorld, and the International Speedway within easy driving distance, Daytona Beach has been a primo Spring Break destination for decades. And it lived up to its billing and more for sparkly, raven-haired Shonelle, a first-year college student with a very advanced grade body.

'MTV was there and everything! It rocked!' she exclaims, waving her fist in the air and grooving, her big boobs bouncing in rhythm. 'I went to all kinds of crazy concerts … and contests: Snoop Dogg and Shaggy; Twister and Spin the Wheel and shit like that. And the club scene was trippin'! The Ocean Deck, Razzle's, 600 North – I par-teed at all of 'em. I even won a wet T-shirt and wet shorty-shorts contest – in one night!'

Shonelle jumps up and spins around, shakes an arse that would be the envy of any fly girl. Then she sits back down, her boobs almost spilling out of her tight, purple tank-top. The girl with the electric smile grins, thinking back to that wet and wild night.

'I forget what club it was,' she says, 'but someone hollered, 'Wet T-shirt contest!' and I was, like, there. It was a total sizzle getting up in front of all those people, my posse cheerin' me on, getting doused with water and bouncing my boobies around. Then they hosed down my booty, and I was shakin' it all over the place. But what happened afterwards was even crazier.'

I only have to wait for the hyper teen to draw a quick breath before she reveals the rest of the story.

'I ran into this washroom backstage to dry off, you know, and the brother who'd been MC-ing the whole thing followed me right inside. At first, I was all ready to kick his black ass, but then I noticed how smokin' hot he was! I guess I hadn't gotten a good look at him on stage.' She sighs, her big, brown eyes gleaming with remembrance. 'He was, like, liquorice dark, with a shaved head and all kinds of muscles. I just stood there and stared at him, my titties all hangin' outta my wet shirt. And he started sweet talkin' me, saying I was the best contestant he'd ever seen and shit like that – really pouring on the sugar, know what I'm sayin'.'

'And he –'

'He sure did.' Shonelle laughs. 'He rolled up my T-shirt and wrung me out like a sponge mop. He put his big hands on my bare titties and started squeezin' 'em real good. Mmmm, it felt evil! Then he started licking my nipples, licking all around and over them. They were popped out rock-hard and electric. And when he started sucking on them, I almost came right there in my panties.'

'But you –'

'Hell, yes! I wanted that stud's big cock inside me, bringin' me off the right away.' Shonelle grins. 'And he buried it deep – and ooooh it felt good. He put me up on the counter and really sexed up the girl, pumping his cock in and out of my coochie. I'd gone full-on a couple of times before, you know, but nothin' like that. This was a man, not a boy, and he knew what he was doin', know what I'm sayin'.'

'And what –'

'I just hung onto his big ol' ass and let him pound me, my tits flyin' all over the place, the music thumping on through the walls. And he jizzed right inside me, shakin' like he was electrocuted or something. Nothin' I could do to stop it – 'cause I was cumming like crazy, too.' Shonelle fans her face with a blinged-up hand. 'That was the best wet T-shirt contest ever!'

South Padre Island, Texas

Located on the Gulf of Mexico, this barrier island with its long, sand-duned beach is well on its way to becoming America's favourite Spring Break party destination. Only 25 miles from Mexico itself, it offers all sorts of fun watersports, such as parasailing and wakeboarding and waterskiing and snorkelling.

And for tall, slim, stunningly blonde Breanne, it offered her a chance to jet ski for the very first time in her life. And a chance to get to know her long-time girlfriend a whole lot better than she'd ever suspected.

'I never in, like, a trillion years would've ever thought Stacey was a lez,' the Maria Sharapova look-a-like confides. 'I mean, we'd gone on tons of double dates together – with guys – rated all the hunks on the football team. I don't know, maybe it's just a phase she's going through or something.' Breanne blushes, confesses, 'And I'm kinda glad I'm going through it with her.'

When pressed for details, the sunny high school senior with the sea-green eyes stares at me for a moment, then swallows hard and provides them.

'Well, we rented this jet ski at that place you recommended. And Stacey drove it around for awhile, with me on the back. It was awesome, like you said it would be – bouncing over the waves, doing donuts, racing other guys. And it was even way more fun when I took the controls. I went, like, full-throttle right away, just about crashed us into this stupid sailboat.'

Breanne giggles, then composes herself and goes on, 'Anyway, I thought maybe I was, like, going too fast for Stacey or something, 'cause she was hugging me so tight – around the waist … at first, at least. Then she moved her hands up higher, 'til they were all the way under my lifejacket and, like, cupping my boobs.'

I glance at the girl's handful breasts, her pointy nipples indenting a 'Got Milk?' T-shirt. And even I get a little moist at the thought of that experimental girl-on-girl scene unfolding out there on the sun-drenched, sparkling green waters of the Gulf.

Breanne rubs her hands on her skintight jeans. 'Well, I slowed right down, of course, 'cause I was, like, all confused about what was going on, you know. But that didn't slow Stacey down. She started full-out groping my boobs – squeezing them and rolling my buds and stuff. I came to a dead-stop in the water and she started kissing my neck, mumbling some junk about how she'd always loved me or whatever.'

The athletic blonde shrugs her buff shoulders, grins a wicked little grin. 'What could I do? I just sat there and took it, sort of watching to make sure no one else came close to us. And I gotta admit, it felt pretty good – the jet ski gently rocking and the sun beating down and Stacey feeling up my boobs and nips. I just sort of leaned back and enjoyed the ride.'

And she enjoyed it still more when her girlfriend-turned-girl-lover unfastened their lifejackets and tossed them overboard, had Breanne turn around and face the sweet music.

'She started kissing me – like boys kiss, 'cept softer.' Breanne closes her eyes and sighs. 'It was really quite wonderful. Then she stuck her hand in my bikini and started rubbing my cunny, while I felt up her boobs, while we frenched like a couple of porn stars. She made me come, like, instantly. I shook so hard I almost fell into the ocean. And then I made her come – with my hand. She gushed all over me!'

When asked if the girls have repeated their Sapphic shenanigans, Breanne nods most emphatically. 'Oh, sure, lots of times. But I'm no lezzy or anything. I'm just, you know, trying to help Stacey through this phase she's going through.'

Lake Havasu, Arizona

Not yet in the same league as Pensacola and Panama City Beach, Florida, Lake Havasu is nonetheless a top Spring Break getaway destination for party-hearty students in the American southwest. A 45-mile-long reservoir formed by the Colorado River, it boasts all the beach, beverage, and water-related activities of its more famous ocean cousins, along with searing desert heat, spectacular mountain scenery, and London Bridge (shipped brick-by-brick from England and reassembled on the spot). And Lake Havasu boasts something else, as well: the hottest teen girl travel sexcapade yet tattled to me.

It comes from Inez, a sultry first-generation Latina with a caramel-coated body that would melt in anyone's mouth. And her tale is all the more surprising considering that her parents are devout churchgoers (I've packaged them up on a couple of trips to the Holy Land myself). Inez claims to live up to their strict standards at home, but on the road, it's a different story.

'It all started, like, so totally innocently,' the brown-eyed eighteen-year-old states, tucking her shiny black locks in behind her ears. 'I was just floating around on this big inner-tube, soaking up the sun and minding my own business.'

She pulls on the hem of her white shorts, her

smooth, brown legs gleaming under the lights. 'And then all of a sudden I felt something, like, tugging on my bikini bottom. I totally freaked! I almost burst the tube with my fingernails. Then I heard someone laughing, and I saw Ken swimming around off to the side. He was smiling and waving at me, so I sorta chilled a bit, thinking he was just having some fun or whatever. But then I felt something slap my bum, and I knew it wasn't him.'

A long-lost legendary water creature like the Loch Ness Monster or Ogopogo? Nope. Only Justin, another frat boy Inez had met at a houseboat party the previous evening.

'Ken and Justin were all yelling at me, teasing me and treading water like crazy. But I just stuck out my tongue and lay back on the tube, playing it real cool. So they started feeling up my bum again – and I mean *really* feeling it up. They squeezed and rubbed and spanked my butt cheeks, pulled my bikini right off. And then someone stuck his tongue in my crack!'

The bright-eyed girl adjusts her tube-top, recrosses her long legs. 'I was, like, totally shocked. I mean, one of them – Ken, I think it was – really spread my cheeks and jammed his tongue right into my bumhole, swirled it around inside me. I didn't know what to do. I mean, there were people floating all around us, on tubes and rafts and boats and whatever. But I don't think anyone saw what was going on – thank God!'

Inez gulps a couple of quick breaths, her perky breasts shuddering.

'So what happened next?'

She stares at me. 'Everything! Ken and Justin start pushing me and my tube towards the beach, up onto the beach. Then they drag me into this little cave they obviously had all picked out ahead of time and …'

Inez blinks. 'You won't tell anyone, will you?'

I shake my head, my fingers working a pencil to the snapping point.

'Well, they both kinda … did me at once,' the teen queen admits. 'They didn't force me or anything like that. Actually, I guess I kinda encouraged them. That tongue slithering up my bum and all the heat and stuff just sorta warped me, I guess. So anyway, Ken stuck his prick in my cun and pumped away while Justin stuck his prick in my mouth and pumped away.' Her eyelids flutter. 'It … was … totally loco! 'Specially for a girl who'd only ever tongue-kissed a guy before.

'But it hardly hurt at all when Ken went … in. And then it just felt totally wicked. I was, like, amazingly hot and wet – getting screwed by one guy and sucking off another.'

I shake my head, my eyes as fiery as Inez's.

'Then, just when I was ready to, like, totally explode – I was tingling sooo bad – Ken and Justin switched places. Justin had a smaller prick, but a slower stroke, like he was more experienced or something. Ken spewed as soon as I wrapped my lips around his knob. 'Course, I was squirting by then, too. And then Justin pulled out and spunked all over my stomach. Which was nice of him, 'cause my parents would absolutely kill me if I ever got pregnant – without being married. I was one sticky, shaky babe by the time we finally crawled back out into the sunshine, let me tell ya!'

So sports fans, take a tip from a lady in the know:

consult with a travel agent before booking your Spring Break vacations, and you just might get something more than cold drinks and hot sun, sand, and surf – you just might get lucky.

For the Love of Arrogance
by Shermaine Williams

TO SAY HE WAS a dislikeable man was an understatement and, officially, I *did* hate him. However, there was still something that drew me to him despite the fact that he was the most egotistical man I had ever met.

If I had my way, I wouldn't be around him at all – honestly – but I was forced to work with him because I was taking over his job as area manager for the bookmakers we worked for. After being promoted, he would be working at head office but I wondered how he was going to cope.

I was going to be making sure all the branches in the area were fully staffed and running smoothly – it was perfect for him. With male members of staff he was the proverbial dick swinger, the big dog who turned up and barked the loudest; with the females, however, it was a completely different story. He was flirtatious, charming and attentive. He was so transparent and, yet, they all seemed to fall for it. I put it down to them being young. I knew better. Yes – I had some weird attraction to him but I would never act on it, I wouldn't give him the satisfaction.

He thrived on attention: wherever he was he swaggered about like he owned the place, it always had to be all eyes on him. To say he was obnoxious was an understatement.

Unbelievably, he had a girlfriend – poor cow! Though I'd never met her, I still felt sorry for her. How did she put up with him?

Being around the guy during the working day was more than enough to satisfy the weird fascination I had with him, but anymore than that would drive me crazy. Maybe she was as bad as him. That must be it: she was one of those high-maintenance types. No doubt they were made for each other and fed off each other's self–importance.

I sat there in the back room, waiting for him, listening to his deep voice as he flirted with the cashier just outside the door.

'Tony,' I called out, finally unable to take any more. 'Can we get on with this?'

'Coming,' he replied sarcastically, after another burst of giggles from the impressionable young woman who held his attention.

'Can't be without me, can you Em?' he smiled, as he walked into the small room.

Being over six feet tall and broad shouldered, his imposing figure seemed to fill the room, making me look tiny by comparison despite being 5'8". It didn't help that I was sitting down as he stalked around the desk to sit next to me. One thing I will say for him is that he always smelt good.

'My name is *Emily* and yes I can,' I insisted, rolling my eyes for good measure. 'Unfortunately, you're the one that knows about this stuff.'

I stared hard at the offending paperwork as if to demonstrate my commitment to it, not wanting to look into his eyes in case he could read something in mine. 'Ah, honey, it's alright to admit that you *need* me.'

Arrogant bastard! I was so outraged that I couldn't think of a clever retort and fell silent. I could feel his eyes boring into me, daring me to look at him. 'Don't be scared to admit it,' he smirked, when I succumbed to my compulsion to look at him.

'I don't need to admit anything!' I finally replied, a little too forcefully.

'I think the lady doth protest too much.'

'Can we just get on with this please?' I knew I sounded exasperated, but I couldn't help it. I desperately hoped my face wasn't as red as it felt as I watched him shrug his acceptance of my suggestion.

The man just made me want to scream.

He kept nudging my arm with his as he tutored me. I had no idea whether he was doing it on purpose and if I said anything I knew he'd make a big deal of it, so I said nothing.

As he finally begun getting serious, I took the opportunity to take surreptitious glances in his direction and couldn't help but wonder what kind of lover he was. I imagined he was quite rough, despite his seemingly charming exterior. It was all an act. In reality, I bet he was the take–charge type who didn't really have that much respect for women. If he had the opportunity, he would probably only use me to get what he wanted, fucking me hard and fast to satisfy himself without giving my pleasure a second thought.

I reckon he loves doggy style – every man loves to see a woman on her hands and knees: he would hold onto my hips and ram his hard, eager cock deep inside me, pulling my hair as he thrust harder and faster …

His mobile rang and jolted me out of my twisted thoughts – thank goodness. I really must be losing my mind.

'It's the little woman,' he announced, looking at the small screen with a mischievous grin on his face. 'You won't get jealous, will you?'

I only narrowed my eyes as I looked at his smug smile; lips that I wanted to kiss on a face that I wanted to slap.

During his call, he slowly paced up and down behind me while I shuffled papers, pretending not to listen as he planned his evening with his girlfriend. I didn't even react on hearing him say: 'I'm with Em' even though it made me wonder if he had spoken to her about me. 'I'm sure she'd love to – I'll ask her.'

Ask me what? After that I just stared blankly at the table, waiting for him to hang up and explain.

'You'll come for a drink after work, won't you Em?'

'Who with?' I asked, trying to sound as innocent as possible.

'Me. But the missus will be there so you'll have to resist the temptation to pounce on me'

'I think I'll manage that just fine.'

The corner of my mouth twitched as he stood grinning at me and I fought to maintain my stern expression as he sat back down so we could resume work.

At no point did I specifically say that I would go and he never asked again, but I knew that I would go and I wondered if he knew that. Was I that transparent?

Did he have that much confidence? In any case, he wasn't the reason I wanted to go; I wanted to meet his girlfriend – the mysterious Nicole.

Tony and I had been working at the same company for months and I know he and Nicole had been together for even longer than that. I only knew of her through gossip and conjecture. I was curious about her and needed to know whether I should feel pity or disdain for her.

As 5.30pm approached, Tony eagerly prepared to leave for the day, despite being just as keen to get to the pub and meet the elusive woman, I did a good job of acting nonchalant as I took my time clearing up and getting my things together.

'Ready?'

Dead on five thirty he was standing by the door; I would have loved to say "I never said I was going" just to see how he'd react, whether his face would drop.

'Sure,' I replied plainly, getting up from my seat.

'Nicole is going to meet us there.'

The pub was a short walk away and I felt really weird walking next to him; having him beside me made me feel powerful, but every time he looked down at me during our conversation I felt small and vulnerable.

I was relieved when we finally turned into the crowded bar. 'There she is.'

I followed his gaze and saw a petite woman at the bar waggling her fingers in our direction and smiling in greeting.

Having been expecting a stern looking Amazonian who could match Tony's stature I couldn't believe this could possibly be her: she was the cutest little woman I had ever seen. How could an idiot like Tony land a woman like that?

'Hi! You must be Emily.' She ignored her boyfriend to greet me first, shaking my hand firmly as her wide smile lit up her face. 'Nice to meet you.'

I instantly liked her.

Her glossy brown fringe skimmed her eyelashes, and each blink caused it to move and catch the light as she held my gaze. Her figure was enviable and I could see why Tony was attracted to her – why any man would be attracted to her – the dark jeans and close fitting top that she wore displayed her curves in a subtle way. I found my gaze lingering a little too long on her breasts which were the perfect size and shape, wondering whether they were real.

'You alright babe?' he asked, leaning down to kiss her tenderly.

I was amazed – he actually seemed like a decent human being. The woman must have magical powers.

With her petite figure and make–up free face, she looked so young and innocent – she had to be several years younger than Tony – that I found myself wondering how these two seemingly polar opposites got together.

Fortunately, Tony was a regular and, after having bought our drinks, wandered off to spread his particular brand of charm, giving me the opportunity to talk to Nicole privately.

I watched her closely as we chatted amiably, expecting her gaze to occasionally stray in Tony's direction, demonstrating some insecurity about his movements, but it never happened. She steadily looked at me as she confidently held up her end of the conversation. I could already tell that she was a genuinely nice woman and, therefore, thought she deserved a better man than the one she had.

'Feel free to tell me to get lost, but can I ask you a question?' I asked tentatively, loath to offend her.

Her hazel eyes widened with curiosity as she nodded, making her fringe tremble and her ponytail flick from side to side. 'Sure?'

'Can't Tony be a bit much?'

With an amused, tight–lipped smile on her face, she furrowed her brow before taking a sip of wine. 'What do you mean?'

'I don't mean to be rude, but he's just so … irritating. How do you cope with him?'

Thankfully, my blunt question only made her laugh, tilting her head back slightly as her eyes twinkled with mirth. 'Ah, he's not that bad.' She turned his way as she spoke and I couldn't quite place the look in her eyes when she turned back to me. I was expecting love or adoration, but it was something else.

'You just don't know him like I do.'

'I reckon you must be a saint.'

She chuckled good–naturedly and I joined her, glad that she hadn't taken offence; not wanting to push it, I changed the subject and we continued to chat as if we were old friends.

'Are you finished hogging my girlfriend?' After a while when Tony had finished doing the rounds, he returned to us and immediately killed the mood with his normal arrogance.

'Hey! Less of that,' she admonished, managing to sound stern and playful at the same time.

'Sorry, sweetheart.' He gazed at her apologetically

for a moment before cocking his head to the side. 'But I want to go – I'm cooking.'

Nicole failed to react to the news and continued to look up at him, a wry smile curling her lips. Tony astonished me by leaning forward to nuzzle her neck, nearly causing her to topple off her barstool. 'Come on,' he almost pleaded.

Despite him acting as if I wasn't there, I was embarrassed to be in the presence of this very public display of affection.

'Stop it,' she ordered, as her hand shot out to grab the bar though she wasn't in any danger of falling.

Tony's hands had travelled up her thighs in order to grip her butt cheeks and he didn't seem keen to let go even with her trying to extricate herself from his embrace, looking exasperated as she shook her head at me over his shoulder. 'Go and wait for me outside.'

For a moment, I actually thought she was talking to me and she spoke so firmly that I actually got off my stool in preparation to follow her instruction.

'See you tomorrow, Em.' Tony immediately straightened up and headed for the door.

'Er … OK, bye.' I was so embarrassed that I tried to cover myself by grabbing my bag as if I was leaving too. 'Don't mind me, I didn't know you had anything planned.'

'We have plans, but just not what you might think.'

She laughed at the confusion she saw on my face. 'I'll tell you what.' She pulled a piece of paper and pen from her bag. 'Why don't you come around and see for yourself – you might see a different side to him.'

'Well, I don't want to disturb you.' I was intrigued but didn't want to impose so had to make a little effort to protest. I was pleased that she continued to jot down their address.

'You won't be – seriously – come round at about eight.'

'OK,' I agreed, accepting the piece of paper.

She smiled in reply before hopping off her stool to hug me, pressing her breasts against me as her soft cheek brushed mine. 'Look forward to seeing you later.'

'Yes … me too,' I replied, surprised to feel her kiss my cheek before we released each other.

After a last wide smile, she followed Tony out of the pub, leaving me wondering what to expect in a few hours time.

I slowed my pace as I approached their front door as I was slightly early and didn't want to be a bad guest – Tony may still be preparing a three–course meal or something. He was probably treated her like a queen: the cockiness was all an act.

Ten minutes early. I didn't consider that too inappropriate so I rang the bell and smoothed my hands over my black pencil skirt.

Presently, the door swung open to reveal Nicole standing there in a loosely tied short black silk robe. I was taken aback: did I have the wrong night? Did I get the time wrong?

'Hi honey,' she smiled, instantly putting my worries to rest.

I let my gaze travel over her body; her cleavage was as impressive as I imagined it to be and with the robe ending at the top of her thighs, it was as if she was daring me not to admire her shapely legs.

'Hi Nicole, am I early?'

'No, you're right on time.' She took my hand to lead me inside as my surprise had left me rooted to the spot.

She kept hold of my hand as we went inside, unable to stop myself from snatching a glance at her high derriere. I think the whole situation had addled my brain a bit as I didn't note that she was leading me to the bedroom until we were actually there and I was stunned to find a very aroused Tony tied to a chair, naked and blindfolded. I had never known his massive frame to look so small.

Wide–eyed and open–mouthed, I stared at Nicole who only smiled seductively as she put her index finger to her lips.

'I'm back, Anthony.'

'Who was at the door?'

'Don't question me!'

'I'm sorry, Mistress.'

I had to cover my mouth to suppress a disbelieving gasp; Nicole smiled broadly, tickled by my expression.

'You're so damn rude.' She walked over and swiped at his cock making it slap against his stomach as he groaned with pain. 'Oh God! I'm sorry, Mistress.'

'I should think so.' If it was possible, I liked her even more. This tiny slip of a woman had this big powerful man completely under her control. 'I'm going to punish you for that.'

I could only stand there enthralled, waiting to see how she would punish him and was confused to see her untying his hands. 'Remember – that cock belongs to me so you better not touch it.'

'Yes Mistress.'

Nicole's tongue darted out to lick her lips as she looked at me with her fingers curling around his blindfold.

'No!' I whispered loudly without thinking.

She ignored me and pulled the scarf away. 'Emily?' He was obviously as surprised to see me there as I was that she had done it at all.

'Excuse me?' Nicole asked curtly, sharply jabbing her fingers against the side of his head.

He looked up at her briefly before turning back to me. 'I'm sorry – Mistress Emily.'

I honestly have no idea how I managed not to burst out laughing at the situation I found myself in.

Her eyes were hard as she looked at him, silently reminding him of the rule, but they softened as she returned to my side, looking me up and down as she approached. 'Relax Emily, let's get you more comfortable.' She slipped my jacket from my shoulders before gently pushing me back until I was forced to sit on the bed. I had no idea what was going to happen and from the panicked look on Tony's face, he didn't either. Standing in front of me, she lightly traced her finger down from my neck and over my breast, making my nipple tingle.

I was speechless and mesmerised as she dropped her robe to expose the matching black lace bra and thong she wore. Her body was stunning, her skin was so smooth I felt as if I wanted to run my fingers over it.

'Have you ever been with a woman?' she asked, interrupting my debauched thoughts.

I could only shake my head.

'I think you'll like it.' As she spoke, she reached

back to unhook her bra, but held it up with her palms on the cups, making sure she still had my undivided attention. She needn't have worried.

I let out an involuntary gasp as she let it drop. Her deep pink nipples looked ripe to be sucked and I couldn't believe that I was willing to oblige. As if reading my mind, she moved forward and offered her gorgeous right tit to my hot, eager mouth. I looked up at her as I teased the erect bud with the tip of my tongue, and was pleased to hear the gratified moan that escaped her lips. I ran my hand up to finger the other nipple as I sucked hungrily. I couldn't believe what I was doing but it felt so good. 'Did you hear what I said?' she suddenly exclaimed, pulling her delicious nipple away, leaving my gaping mouth wanting. 'Didn't I tell you not to touch your cock?'

Having been watching proceedings, Tony had been unable to resist and Nicole had caught him fondling his rigid shaft.

'I'm sorry, Mistress,' he said, looking at her anxiously. 'Please … don't.'

'I'm not going to – Mistress Emily will.'

Me? What was I going to do? To get the answer, I kept my eyes on Nicole who walked over to collect a black paddle that hung on the back of the door. She pulled me to my feet and handed it to me, allowing me to stroke my thumb over the cool smoothness of the leather as she leaned forward to gently press her lips against mine. My first kiss from a woman. Her lips were so soft I felt like I could melt into them and boldly slid my tongue between her lips, hearing Tony groan as we kissed passionately.

I wondered if she heard it too as her hands travelled

around my back to unzip my skirt. I gasped into her mouth as her fingers brushed against the small of my back. She pulled away from me to look in Tony's direction, causing him to hurriedly move his hands away form his crotch. 'Get over here,' she said hoarsely.

He immediately did as he was told and was soon towering over the dominant woman. 'Get on the bed – on your hands and knees.'

His hard cock bounced as he got into position. 'Stay still and don't say a word.'

As soon as she was satisfied that he would do as she said she turned her attention back to me, firmly placing her hands on my hips to turn me around before – keeping her eyes on mine – kneeling in front of me and taking my skirt with her. I'd begun to get wet when I tasted her luscious nipple and I was strangely embarrassed about her realising this as her fingers worked their way up my inner thigh; however, she didn't seem fazed and I sighed with pleasure as she lightly pressed her thumb against my clit through my damp knickers. 'You're going to spank him while I taste you.'

It wasn't a request and I wouldn't have been able to refuse even if it had been; I moved my legs closer together to aid her removal of my underwear.

She stroked the backs of my thighs as I looked up at Tony's pale arse in front of me. I had never spanked anyone before and felt weird being in the position to do so.

'Do it,' Nicole whispered, as she threw my knickers aside and spread my legs.

Her lips were so close, only a few inches and she'd

be able to slide her tongue into my cleft. I so wanted to feel it.

Tony was trembling, but I cared more about my own feelings and slapped the thick leather against his skin knowing it would please Nicole. He flinched and sharply took in a breath but I barely noticed because I was being rewarded. She tickled my clit hood with the tip of her tongue before firmly licking my clit.

Oh God! She was so good.

I raised my arm and hit him again, barely seeing the red mark that my first hit had caused. She took my clit into her warm mouth and made me moan. I wanted to run my fingers through her hair, but I had a job to do.

The next strike was harder – enough to make him whimper – but it had the desired effect and Nicole gripped my butt cheeks and buried her mouth against my pussy.

As she thrust her tongue into my pussy, I knew I was lost and would do anything to make her continue; I spanked Tony with reckless abandon, landing blow after blow in quick succession, his cheeks becoming increasingly red as I submitted to the pleasure I was feeling.

Even with my moaning and Tony's gasps of pain, the crack of leather against skin could clearly be heard. I ground my pubis against her face as the pressure began to build and I frenziedly beat him so that she would make me come. Tony had the same idea and his body shuddered before his arms buckled and he collapsed on the bed, leaving me free to discard the paddle for the sake of holding Nicole's head, fucking her mouth until the orgasm hit and radiated throughout my body from my clit.

My legs trembled as she lapped up my juices.

Sitting in the back room the next morning, I felt contented and relieved: I wasn't attracted to the annoying man, I just wanted to dominate him.

His entrance made me jump as I hadn't heard him arrive – definitely a first – and I boldly looked at him as he looked at me sheepishly. 'Hello Emily.'

I had never know him to be so quiet; no wisecracks, no teasing, nothing. He could barely look me in the eye. 'Hello Anthony.'

I continued to look at him steadily, daring him to meet my gaze.

His mobile rang and broke the battle of wills; I snatched it up before he had a chance. Seeing Nicole's name caused a distinct tingling to develop between my thighs. 'It's the little woman,' I smiled, looking up at him from beneath my lashes. 'Don't get jealous, will you?'

I pressed the button to answer the call.

Also from Xcite Books

Ultimate Uniforms
Miranda Forbes

Ultimate Uniforms

If a commanding man or imperious woman dressed in a smart uniform makes your heart tick faster, these 20 original stories exploring the sensual delights of uniforms, both for the wearer and the admirer, are guaranteed to seize your attention.

Whether it is the smartness and authority of military dress, the sassy temptations of a naughty maid, or the possibilities offered by a policewoman, arousing descriptions and unabashed accounts of kinky sexual encounters await!

ISBN 9781907761324 £7.99

Kinky Girls
An Xcite Collection of Women on the Wild Side
Miranda Forbes

Kinky Girls

Women who act on their most shameful fantasies and embark upon the most daring misbehaviour, is still the most enduring and timeless theme in erotic fantasy, and loved by male and female readers alike. And this collection takes the idea of a kinky adventurous woman to the max. A collection of 20 original, varied, outrageous, eye-watering and utterly sensuous stories from the best new voices and established authors around today.

ISBN 9781907016561 £7.99

The Education of Victoria
Angela Meadows

The Education of Victoria
Angela Meadows

Lessons in love and a whole lot more are in store in this saucy romp set in a European finishing school for young ladies.

Packed off to a continental finishing school, 16-year-old Victoria thinks she will be taught how to be a dutiful wife for a gentleman. But she soon finds she has a lot to learn in the arts of pleasure at the Venus School for Young Ladies.

There she encounters the strictness of Principal Madame Thackeray and her team of tutors. Under their guidance she learns the finer arts of sexual pleasure and discovers that there are plenty of fellow students and staff willing to share carnal knowledge with this sweet English rose.

On returning to England, she finds her father in financial difficulty and must turn her newfound education to good use to survive.

ISBN 9781906373696 £7.99

The true
confessions
of a
London
Spank
Daddy
PETER JONES

The True Confessions of a London Spank Daddy
Peter Jones

Discover an underworld of sex, spanking and submission. A world where high-powered executives and cuddly mums go to be spanked, caned and disciplined.

In this powerful and compelling book Peter Jones reveals how his fetish was kindled by corporal punishment while still at school and how he struggled to contain it. Eventually, he discovered he was far from alone in London's vibrant, active sex scene.
Chapter by chapter he reveals his clients' stories as he turns their fantasies into reality. The writing is powerful, the stories graphic and compelling.

Discover an unknown world …

ISBN 9781906373320 £7.99